THE CHILD'S BOOK OF NATURE: PLANTS

This edition published 2026
by Living Book Press
Copyright © Living Book Press, 2026

ISBN: <<ISBN_HC>> (hardcover)
         <<ISBN_SC>> (softcover)

First published in 1882.

This edition is based on the 1882 printing by Harper & Brothers.

A catalogue record for this book is available from the National Library of Australia

The Child's Book
of Nature: Plants

WORTHINGTON HOOKER

CONTENTS

CHILDREN ARE busy observers of natural objects, and have many questions to ask about them. But their inquisitive observation is commonly repressed, instead of being encouraged and guided. The chief reason for this unnatural course is, that parents and teachers are not in possession of the information which is needed for the guidance of children in the observation of nature. They have not themselves been taught aright, and therefore are not able to teach others. In their own education the observation of nature has been almost entirely excluded; and they are, therefore, unprepared to teach a child in regard to the simplest natural phenomena.

Here is a radical error in education. When we put a child into the school-room, to be drilled in spelling, reading, arithmetic, geography, etc., we effectually shut him in from all the varied and interesting objects of nature, which he is so naturally inclined to observe and study. These are very seldom made the subjects of instruction in childhood. And even at the fireside the deficiency is nearly as great as it is in the school-room.

A similar defect appears to a great extent through the whole course of education. The study of the wonderful phenomena which are all around us and within us, is, for the most part, neglected, except by the few whose inclinations to it are so strong that they can not be repressed. This defect is well illustrated in a remark which was made by a mother in relation to her own education. When at school she stood at the head of her class, and excelled particularly in mathematics. Her remark was, that she every day regretted that much of the time she had given to the study of mathematics had not been spent in learning what would enable her to answer the continual questions of her children. Even when the natural sciences are taught, the mode of teaching them is generally ineffectual. The knowledge which the mass of pupils in our higher schools gain of Natural Philosophy, Chemistry, Botany, and Physiology, is very deficient.

There should be a thorough change in this respect in the whole course of education, beginning in childhood. The natural sciences should be made prominent among the studies even of young children, who, in other words, should be encouraged and guided in that observation of nature to which they are generally so much inclined. In the different departments of natural science there are multitudes of facts or phenomena in which children readily become interested, when they are properly explained.

In this little book my object is to supply the mother and the teacher with the means of introducing the child into one department of natural science—that which relates to the vegetable world,or vegetable physiology. With this view, I have endeavored to select those points only which the child will fully understand, and in which he will be interested. But this selection has by no means shut me up within narrow limits. I have been surprised at the amount of knowledge in this interesting study that can be satisfactorily communicated to the mind of a child. While the fundamental points in vegetable physiology are quite fully developed in this book, I have avoided as far as possible all technical terms. These can be learned when the pupil becomes old enough to profit by learning them. The facts, the phenomena, are what the child wants to understand; and these can be communicated in the simplest language, so that a child of about seven or eight, or perhaps even six years, can readily be made to comprehend them.

I begin with the most simple and obvious facts—those which relate to flowers—and go on through fruits, seeds, leaves, roots, etc., step by step, until, at the latter part of the book, the circulation of the sap, and other points at first view complicated, are made perfectly intelligible. By this gradual unfolding of the subject, many points are made clear to the child, which are not fully understood by many of those who in riper years have studied botany; for in the common mode of teaching this science the mere technicalities of it are made prominent, while the interesting facts which vegetable physiology presents to us in such variety receive but little attention.

The best time to use this book in teaching is during the summer, because then every thing can be illustrated by specimens from the field and the garden, and the teacher can amplify upon what I have given. For example, when the lesson is to be on leaves, the teacher can request her scholars to bring as many different kinds of leaves as they can find; and she can point out their differences after the same plan that I have adopted, but in a much more extended manner. Indeed, if the teacher catch herself the true spirit of observation, she will be continually led in her teachings to add facts of her own gathering to those which I have presented.

I believe that there are few terms in the book that can not be readily understood by the child. A little explanation may sometimes be necessary on the part of the teacher, especially when the same word is used as meaning more at one time than at another. For example, the word plant is used sometimes, as in the title of this book, to include every thing that is vegetable; while at another time it is used to distinguish certain forms of vegetables from others, as in the expression plants and trees.

I have made such a division into chapters as will place each subject by itself, and at the same time, for the most part, give lessons of a proper length for the learner. I have placed questions at the end of each chapter, for convenience in instruction. Of course the teacher or parent will vary them as she sees fit, to accommodate the capacities of those whom she teaches.

WORTHINGTON HOOKER.

CHAPTER I.

OUR LOVE FOR FLOWERS.

EVERY BODY likes flowers. We like them wherever we see them. How pleasant they are to our eyes as we see them in the garden! How their various colors please us as we look along the borders! Some are red, some are white, some are blue, and some are yellow. All these different colors, mingled with the fresh green leaves, make a feast for our eyes.

And then we love to look at each flower by itself. Some flowers we like better than we do others. A pretty little flower that smells sweet, we like better than we do a large one that has no perfume. The peony is very beautiful, but we do not love it as we do the little pink with its delightful fragrance.

It was a garden in which Adam and Eve were placed. While they were innocent and pure God surrounded them with beautiful things, because he loved them so much. Before they sinned they lived among the flowers and trees of the garden of Eden. It was more beautiful than any garden that has been seen since that time. It was so beautiful that God would not let Adam and Eve stay in it after they had sinned.

As we roam about the fields and the woods, it is pleasant to see here and there a flower. We should hardly enjoy our walk if we did not see them. They are like familiar friends that we love to meet. We see them come every year after the winter is gone, and we like to bid them welcome. A little girl, finding a wild violet early in the spring, exclaimed, "How glad I am to see you again! It is a long time since I have seen you, and you look as pretty as ever!" The delight expressed by this little girl is felt by every body that loves flowers, as they come one after another in the spring. How much we should miss them if they did not come every year!

The earliest flowers that we see in the spring are the most precious to us. They are very welcome, coming so soon after the cold winter is gone. They are the first children of spring. They are few. We find them only here and there. But we know that there will be many more flowers as the warm summer comes on; and we rejoice to greet the first of the host of beautiful things that are to delight our eyes in the field and in the garden.

These early flowers that we love so much are very little flowers. Look at the sweet little flowers of the trailing arbutus as they peep out from among its rough leaves. It seems as if they scarcely dared to show themselves, for fear that old winter had hardly gone. The violets too, are small, and just lift their heads from the ground. So, too, the delicate anemones, that are moved by the least breath of air, are very small.

We are so fond of flowers that we like to have them where we can look at them in the winter. We are not willing to wait till spring comes. So we keep them in our warm rooms on stands at the windows. Those who can afford it sometimes have green-houses, in order that they may keep a great variety of plants, and have flowers all the time.

People sometimes become very much attached to a few plants that they keep in their windows. Their opening flowers seem to smile upon them, and this is very pleasant to them in the midst of the dreariness of winter. It makes a little summer for them in-doors. And if the plants happen to get frozen some very cold night, it makes them feel really quite sad. A little girl became very much attached to a plant given to her by her mother. She watered it every day, and watched the buds on it as they opened into flowers. It was one of her pets. But one night it froze, and the little girl wept over her loss. She felt as if she had lost a sweet and ever-smiling friend. A kind neighbor gave her another plant of the same kind; but it was a long time before she could feel that it was just as good as the one that she had lost.

There is a beautiful story in French of a prisoner who became exceedingly attached to a flower. He was put in prison by Napoleon because he was supposed to be an enemy of the government. One day as Charney (for that was his name) was walking in the yard adjoining his cell, he saw a plant pushing up from between the stones. How it came there he could not tell. Perhaps some one carelessly dropped the seed. Or perhaps the seed was blown over the wall by the wind. He knew not what plant it was, but he felt a great interest in it. Shut in within those walls away from all his friends, not permitted to interest himself with either reading or writing, he was glad to have this little living thing to watch over and love. Every day when he walked in the court he spent much time in looking at it. He soon saw some buds. He watched them as they grew larger and larger, and longed to see them open. And when the flowers at length came out he was filled with joy. They were very beautiful. They had three colors in them—white, purple, and rose color; and there was a delicate silvery fringe all round the edge. Their fragrance, too, was delicious. Charney examined them more than any he had ever seen before; and never did flowers look so beautiful to him as these.

Charney guarded his plant with great care from all harm. He made a frame-work out of such things as he could get, so that it should not be broken down by some careless foot or by the wind. One day there was a hail-storm; and to keep his tender plant from the pelting of the hail, he stood bending over it as long as the storm lasted.

The plant was something more than a pleasure and a comfort to the prisoner. It taught him some things that he had never learned before, though he was a very wise man. When he went into the prison he was an atheist. He did not believe there was a God; and among his scribblings on the prison wall he had written, "All things come by chance." But as he watched his loved flower, its opening beauties told him that there is a God. He felt that none but God could make that flower. And he said that the flower had taught him more than he had ever learned from the wise men of the earth.

The cherished and guarded plant proved of great service to the prisoner. It was the means of his being set free. I will tell you how this was. There was another prisoner, an Italian, whose daughter came to visit him. She was much interested by the tender care which Charney took of his plant. At one time it seemed as if it were going to die, and Charney felt very sad. He wished that he could take up the stones around it, but he could not without permission. The Italian girl managed to see the Empress Josephine, and to tell her about it; and permission was given to Charney to do with his plant as he desired. The stones were taken up, and the earth was loosened, and the flower was soon as bright as ever again.

Now Josephine thought much of flowers. It is said that she admired the purple of her cactuses more than the Imperial purple of her robe, and that the perfume of her magnolias was pleasanter to her than the flattery of her attendants. She, too, had a cherished flower—the sweet jasmine, that she had brought from the home of her youth, a far-off island of the West Indies. This had been planted and reared by her own hand; and though its simple beauty would scarcely have excited the attention of a stranger, it was dearer to her than all the rare and brilliant flowers that filled her hot-houses. She thought a good deal, therefore, of the prisoner that took such care of his one flower. She inquired about him, and after a little time persuaded the Emperor to give him his freedom. And when Charney left the prison he took the plant with him to his home; for he could not bear to part with this sweet companion that had cheered him in his lonely prison life, taught him such lessons of wisdom, and was at last the means of setting him free.

Some, perhaps, would say that the seed of this flower got into that prison-yard, and took root in the earth between the stones by *chance*, and that this was all very *lucky* for the prisoner. But this is not so. Nothing comes by chance. God sent that seed there, and made it lodge in the right place to have it grow. He sent it to do great things for the poor prisoner. Little did Charney think, when he saw that tiny plant first pushing up from between the stones, that by it God would free him from prison, and, what was better, deliver him from his infidelity.

Questions.—*What* is said of our love for flowers? Do we like some flowers better than others? What is said of the garden of Eden? How do we feel about the wild flowers of spring? Why do we like the earliest best? Are these large or small? Mention some of them. Why do people keep flowers in the winter in their rooms and in green-houses? Tell about the little girl and her plant. What is the story of the French prisoner and his plant?

CHAPTER II.
MORE ABOUT OUR LOVE FOR FLOWERS.

IT IS from our love of flowers that a bouquet is always a pretty present to a friend. The kind teacher is much gratified when a scholar, with a bright, cheerful "Good morning," gives her a bouquet. Though the flowers may be simple and common, the present is a very pleasant one. It is saying to your teacher, I love the beautiful things that God has made, and I know that you love them. It is saying more than this. It is telling your teacher that you love her. It is because you love her that you give her the sweet flowers that you love so much. And she will feel that though the flowers will fade, your love to her will ever be fresh.

How grateful are flowers in the chamber of sickness! It would weary the sick one to see all her kind friends. But they can send her presents to let her know that they think of her. And what tokens of remembrance are more welcome than flowers?

Flowers are much used as ornaments, even among savages. They are more beautiful than any ornaments that man can make. What is more elegant than handsome hair dressed with flowers?

As natural flowers droop so easily, we make artificial ones for ornaments. Sometimes they are made so well that they look like fresh flowers just picked from the garden.

We like flowers so much that we copy them in the figures in dress and furniture. Gems and ornaments of gold and silver are arranged in flower-shapes. Figures of flowers are seen in the patterns on dresses more often than any other figures. The calico-printer gets his prettiest figures from the flowers that he sees in the field and garden. The richest carpets are those in which the figures are flowers. We often see in the carpet under our feet a great variety of flowers of the most beautiful colors. We seem to tread on beds crowded full of roses and various kinds of flowers; and we have no fear of crushing them as when we tread on real flowers. Flowers, too, are stamped on the papers on our walls. You often see representations of flowers woven in table-cloths and napkins. You see the figures of flowers worked beautifully on articles of silver. You see them too on vases in which we put real flowers. Flowers are often carved in furniture, and even the stove-maker has them on his stoves, whether they are made for the parlor or the kitchen. Thus it is that we have flowers about us whenever we can. And where we can not have flowers, we have rep-resentations of them.

I said in the first chapter that every body likes flowers. Perhaps I ought to say that *almost* every body likes them. A man may be so wicked and so like a brute that he can see no beauty in flowers. A man may love to hoard up money, so much, that he will not care about any thing beautiful. Some men can not see any use in flowers. They think that potatoes, and turnips, and beets, ought to grow where their daughters have their flower-garden. They forget that God has given us beautiful things for the purpose of having us enjoy them. God has a use for every thing that he has made, and this is the use of flowers. And he likes to see us love the beautiful things that he has given us, and make a proper use of them.

Children always love flowers. The baby puts out its little hands to them before it can hold any thing, and shows that it is pleased by its smiles and funny noises. And the child that can run about and talk, is delighted as it runs up and down the garden, and says "Pretty, pretty!" to every flower.

There ought always to be flowers in the school-room. The place where the happy child goes to learn should be made very cheerful. Pleasant things will make it so, and flowers are certainly very pleasant things. And then, they are very easily obtained. Scholars can bring them, and they can be put into vases where all can see them. Pictures would make a school-room look very pleasant, but they are too costly. Flowers are cheap, since they commonly cost only the trouble of gathering and bringing them to school.

Questions.—*What* is said about giving a bouquet to your teacher? Why are presents of flowers so pleasant to a sick person? What is said of flowers as ornaments? What of artificial flowers? Tell how we copy flowers in dress and in furniture. Are there some who do not like flowers? For what did God make flowers? How do very little children show that they like them? What is said about having flowers in the school-room?

CHAPTER III.

HOW FLOWERS ARE MADE.

IF YOU love flowers you will like to know all that you can about them. It is just as it is when you love a person. You want to know all that you can about the friends that you love so well. And if you love flowers, you will like to know what I have to tell you about them.

You go out into the garden, and you see among all the flowers there a large red rose. Look at it, and see how many red leaves it has all folded together. How did that rose come there? That is plain enough, you will say—it *grew* there. And most grown people as well as children think that this is all that is to be said about it. But what is *growing*? Do you know *how* a rose grows? I will tell you something about this.

That rose was once a very little bud, such as you see here. Then it did not look any thing like a rose. It was a little green thing with nothing red in it. You would not suppose that it ever could turn into a rose, if you had not seen buds turn into roses before.

The little rose-bud becomes larger and larger every day. Soon it begins to open, as is represented here, and you see the red leaves of the flower all folded together. It spreads out these leaves after a little time, and now you see the full-blown rose.

Here is a representation of a rose in full bloom. How much larger it is than the little bud from which it came, and how different it is from it! A great many leaves it spreads out in its bosom. Sometimes the difference is greater than what you see here. Some kinds of roses are very large indeed, but their buds at the first are very small.

This rose was *made*. We commonly say that it grew, without thinking what growing is. It was made from something. There was something that came to the bud to make it into a rose. What was it that came to the bud? How did it come there? I will tell you.

The rose was made from a juice, or *sap*, as we call it. This sap kept coming to the bud all the time that it was growing larger, and then all the time that it was changing into a rose. We do not know *how* this sap can be made into such a beautiful red flower. This we can not understand. The wisest man in the world can not tell us how it is done. But God, who made all the flowers and every thing else, understands it.

But you will ask how the sap comes to the bud. You see that slender stem that holds the rose. There are little fine pipes in that stem, and the sap comes through these pipes. All the time that the bud is turning into a rose, the sap comes to it through these pipes in the stem, just as water comes through pipes to our houses. These pipes in the stem are very small, and there are a great many of them. They are so small that you can not see them, but they are large enough to let the sap run along through them.

If the sap should stop coming through these pipes to the bud, it could not become a rose. If you pick a bud, you know that it stops growing, and never becomes a rose. This is because no more sap can come to it through the pipes of the stem. It is just as no water can come into a house if the water-pipe be cut off outside.

The sap from which the rose is made we should suppose would be like the rose. But it is not. It is not red, as you see breaking the stem. It does not taste at all like the leaves of the rose.

It does not seem very wonderful that the little green bud should be made from the sap in the stem. But it does seem very strange that the bright-red leaves of the rose should be made from it. Suppose some one should take some stems, and bruise them, so as to get the sap out of them. Could he make a rose from this sap? Oh no. This can be done only in the bud. That is the rose-factory. The sap must go there to be made into a rose.

Questions.—*Why* do you want to know about flowers? Do most people think it plain how a rose-bud becomes a rose? How is the rose different from the bud? Is the rose made? What is it made from? How does the sap get to the bud? If you pick a bud, why does it not become a rose? Is the sap in the stem like the rose? Can any one make a rose from the sap?

CHAPTER IV.

THE COLORS OF FLOWERS.

I HAVE told you about red roses. But all roses, you know, are not red. There are white and yellow roses. And some roses are a very light red, while others are a dark red. Now, how are all these different colors made?

If you ask a dyer how he gives cloths different colors, he will tell you that he dips them into different dyes. He has a dye in one place that gives a red color, and one in another place that gives a yellow color; and so for all the different colors. The roses are not colored in this way; they are not dipped into dyes. But the colors must come from something. From what do you think they come?

We do not know exactly how these colors are made. The sap seems to be the same in the stems of all the different roses. It is not yellow in the stem of the yellow rose, and red in the stem of the red rose. The stems of all the roses are green, and the buds at first are green. But in some way all the different colors are made from something. And as there is nothing there but the sap that comes in the stems, the colors must be made from this. Air and light have something to do with making the colors, but they are made from the sap.

I have told you only about roses. But there are many, very many other flowers with every variety of color. They are all made from the sap that comes to the buds through the stems. This is true of the flowers on the trees as well as of those that you see on stalks and bushes.

The sap is different in the different trees and plants. But

in none of them can you find sap that is like the flowers that are made from it.

In some flowers you see different colors beautifully mixed together. These different colors are made from the same sap. In the garden-violet you see a purple and a yellow color. In the iris you see a purple, a yellow, and a blue. These three colors are very unlike, and yet they are made from the same sap that comes up the stem. In the China pinks you see a great variety of colors alongside of each other.

Sometimes the colors shade off into each other beautifully. You see this in the pink. Sometimes one color is put right upon another in streaks or in spots. You see stripes of color in tulips. In the tiger lily there are dark spots of a very different color from that reddish-brown upon which they are put.

How it is that out of the same sap one color is made in one part of a flower, and another color in another part, we do not know. Sometimes two entirely different colors are side by side. In one kind of poppy the leaves of the flower are white except on the very end, and there they are red. They look as if all their edges had been dipped in a red dye. Now how it is that the sap should make the flower white every where except on the tips of its leaves, and there make it red, we do not know.

Neither can we tell how one color is made to shade off or run into another color. This is often so nicely done, that you can not tell where one color begins and another ends. You see this in the apple-blossom. The reddish color runs off into a pure white, but there is no place where you can say the white begins.

The colors of flowers change some as they open. A flower is not exactly of the same color when it is partly opened as it is when its leaves are all spread out to the light. There is a vine called the cobea that has a singular change in the color of its flowers. When they first open they are a pale green. They are of this color when they are fully opened. But after a while they have a rich purple color. It is like the change of color that you see in some fruits. An orange, you know, is at first green; but when it is ripe, it is a bright yellow orange.

I might go on to tell you much more about the colors of flowers. But you can look for yourselves in the garden and in the field, and see how differently the colors are arranged in one flower and in another.

Questions.—Are roses of different colors? How does a dyer give different colors to cloth? Do we know how the colors of flowers are made? What are they made from? What is said of the great variety of colors in flowers? Mention some flowers in which different colors are alongside of each other. Is it strange that they are made from the same sap? What is said of one kind of poppy? What is said of the shading off of colors? Tell about the flower of the cobea.

CHAPTER V.

THE PERFUME OF FLOWERS.

THERE IS another thing in the flower besides the color that is made from the sap. It is its perfume. How delightful this is in the rose! And how long it lasts! But you can smell none of it in the sap from which the rose is made. There is commonly very little odor in the stem through which the sap comes to a flower, and it is not at all like that which you smell in the flower itself.

The perfume is not in the stem; but that from which the perfume is made is there. Something is done to the sap as it comes to the flower to make it give out the perfume. Every fragrant flower is a *perfume-factory*.

Some flowers have no odor, while others smell very strong. The lilac and the syringa, you know, have a strong smell. They are quite pleasant in the open air; but when they are in a closed room they are disagreeable, because their odor is so strong.

There is no fragrance in many of our most beautiful flowers. This is true of the cactus in all its varieties. When you look at a large cactus blossom, so splendid in its colors, it seems to you that it must smell sweet. But if you put it to your nose, as a child is apt to do, you find that it has no smell. Then there are the elegant japonicas, of various colors, that have no fragrance. The showy red peonies in the garden look to a child so much like large red roses, that it seems to him as if they ought to have a pleasant smell. But they have none. Perhaps you have seen in the autumn some very bright scarlet flowers standing on a stalk in damp places. It is the cardinal flower. Some call it eye-bright. This elegant flower has no fragrance. And there is none in the fringed gentian, another beautiful wild flower of autumn. It seems enough for such flowers that they are so beautiful.

But there are some flowers that have both great beauty and delicious fragrance. This is true of most kinds of roses. Whenever any one gives you a rose, you put it up to your nose at once. You expect that it will smell sweet, of course; and you feel disappointed if it does not. The cape jessamine is one of the most beautiful of flowers, and, at the same time, it has a delightful fragrance. The pure clear white flower appears very beautiful among the glossy green leaves. In a southern climate it is one of the most splendid of flowers.

Most flowers have some odor. And the odors of the different flowers are all different from each other. If you were blindfolded, and a pink, a rose, an apple blossom, a pond lily, an orange blossom, and a clover-head, were put up to your nose, one after the other, you would know each of them by its smell. And so of other flowers. What a variety there is in the fragrance that the flowers in the garden and the field send forth into the air! What a multitude of different perfume-factories has our kind heavenly Father provided just to gratify us!

Sometimes a great many of these factories of one kind are together, and then the air is filled with the perfume they make. You will at once think of a clover-field. How sweet the fragrance as the wind blows over the field and brings it to you! All this perfume comes from millions of little factories. For each clover-head is a perfume-factory, as you may know if you pick one and smell it.

The fragrance from the flowers of the grape-vine is very delicious. It is of this that Solomon speaks when he says, "The vines with the tender grape give a good smell." When the grape-vines are in bloom the air is filled with their fragrance; and yet the flowers are so small, and so near the color of the stem and the leaves, that you would not notice them, unless you looked particularly for them.

There are some flowers that have an unpleasant odor. Sometimes this is because they are poisonous, the odor making us avoid them, and thus saving us from danger. But in many cases we can not see any such reason for the unpleasant odor. Why it is that such a splendid flower as the crown imperial should smell so disagreeable we do not understand. One thing, however, is true: the bad-smelling plants are few, while God has given us a multitude of those that smell sweet.

Questions.—*What* else in the flower, besides color, is made from the sap? Is the perfume in the stem? Where is it made? Mention some flowers that have a strong smell. Mention some that are very handsome, and yet have no fragrance. Mention some that have both fragrance and beauty. What is said about the different odors of flowers? How does this show the goodness of God to us? Tell about the clover-field. What is said of the flowers of the grape-vine? What is said of flowers with a bad odor?

CHAPTER VI.

THE SHAPES OF FLOWERS.

FLOWERS ARE of all kinds of shapes. The shape of the flower often gives it its name. Some are shaped like stars, and are called asters, the word in Latin for stars. There are many kinds of these asters that grow wild in the autumn. Some of them are blue, some purple, and some white. And then there are the China-asters that you see in the garden.

There is a beautiful wild flower called, from its shape, ladies' tresses. And so, too, we have ladies' ear-drops, and the lady's slipper.

Some flowers are shaped like butterflies. This is the shape of the pea-blossom which you see here. A very beautiful flower it is, though people seldom think much about it. They think only of the peas which they are to gather by-and-by. There is one curious thing about the color of the pea-blossom. Sometimes, you know, it is white, and some-

times it is a purplish red. Now when it is red, you can see red spots all the way down the stalk, at the joints where the branches go off from it. It is as if the sap as it went up to color the blossom, left some of its red dye in these spots on the way. You see no such spots on the stalk when the flowers are white.

Here are the flowers of the

lily of the valley. They are like little bells hanging from the stem. This is one of the sweetest of all flowers. The little blue-bells, so pretty, and yet so troublesome in the garden, have their name from their bell-shape. So also have the Canterbury bells.

Some flowers are cup-shaped. This shape gives its name to the bright yellow buttercup that you know so well. The cup-daffo-dil, as we call it, has the middle part of the flower in the shape of a cup. The cup part of it is quite deep. The flower is bent over. If it stood upright, its cup would be filled with water when it rains. The narcissus, too, which bends

over like the cup-daffodil, has a little cup, as you see in the figure, in the middle of it. Its cup, you observe, is shallow. It is something like a bowl.

Here is a flower of a funnel or tunnel shape. We see this shape in the flowers of the cypress-vine, and of the tobacco-plant. The flower of the morning-glory, which you will see on page 41, has this shape quite perfectly. It looks very much like a tunnel.

The flower that you see here is one of the varieties of calceolaria. It hangs down like a bag, or pocket, having a round opening above. The blossom of which this is a drawing was of a bright yellow color with red spots on it. There are many varieties

of this singular flower, having different colors, and different sizes.

The flower here represented is the wake-robin, or Indian turnip. It is found in rather damp and shady places. What you see is commonly called the flower, but it is not really so. It is a covering for the flowers of the plant, which are very small. They are on the lower part of that rounded

stalk that stands up in the middle. This splendid covering or house for the little flowers is green in one variety, and of a dark purple in the other. In the beautiful calla the flowers are small, and are on a stalk like that in the wake-robin. That pure white trumpet-shaped thing that we so much admire is not really the flower, though it is called so.

Some flowers are shaped like a trumpet. This is the shape of the blossom of the trumpet-creeper. The blossom, you know, is very deep. The humming-bird is fond of going quite into it. I suppose he goes in after the honey in the bottom of the flower. I have sometimes caught this beautiful bird by grasping the blossom in my hand when he had fairly got into it. I only kept the trembling little creature long enough to let us see how beautiful he was, and how curiously his long bill was made, with its slender tongue, to gather the honey. I soon set him free, and he was off again as joyous and as busy as ever, going from flower to flower.

The blossom of the snap-dragon has a queer shape that gives it its name. By pressing it together sideways, you can make it open like a mouth, and there are little white things that look like teeth. And then, if you let go of it, this mouth snaps together.

You have often seen the golden rod by the road-side in the last of summer and in autumn. Its golden yellow blossoms grow on a tall stalk in such a way that its name seems a very proper one. It is truly a rod of golden flowers.

There are some flowers that are called *compound*. They are called so because each flower is made up of a great many flowers. The dandelion is a flower of this kind. Each blossom has a great number of flowers in it. These you can easily pick apart. Each one of these looks beautiful if you see it through a microscope.

The blossom of the clover is one of the same kind of flowers. The white daisy, too, or ox-eyed daisy, as some call it, that you see scattered over fields among the grass, is a compound flower. I have counted in one of these blossoms over six hundred flowers.

These flowers are in the yellow part in the middle, that

has a row of white leaves all around it. They are very small. But when you look at them through a micro-scope, you can see that each one is a beautiful, perfect flower. So, then, there is a whole garden of flowers in one of these blossoms. If these six hundred flowers could be taken out and turned into large flowers, they would make very much such a show as six hundred yellow lilies would.

The mountain daisy, here represented, is a pretty little flower of the same kind. It has in its golden yellow bosom a multitude of little flowers close together, just as our common white daisy has. And around this yellow part there is a row of delicate leaves, sometimes reddish, and sometimes white. This is a favorite flower in England and Scotland, where it is very common in the fields. There has been a great deal of poetry written about it. Burns, the great poet of Scotland, has some sweet verses to this "wee, modest, crimson-tipped flower," as he calls it. Here are some lines that some one has written about it.

> "I'm a pretty little thing,
> Always coming with the spring;
> In the meadows green I'm found,
> Peeping just above the ground,
> And my stalk is covered flat
> With a white and yellow hat.
>
> "Little maiden, when you pass
> Lightly o'er the tender grass,
> Step aside, and do not tread
> On my meek and lowly head,
> For I always seem to say,
> Chilly winter's gone away."

Very pretty poetry this is, but I think the poet is wrong in making this modest little flower praise itself.

The flowers on many trees hang down, as represented in this figure, in tassels. The flowers of the willow hang in this way. There are a great many flowers in each tassel. In the

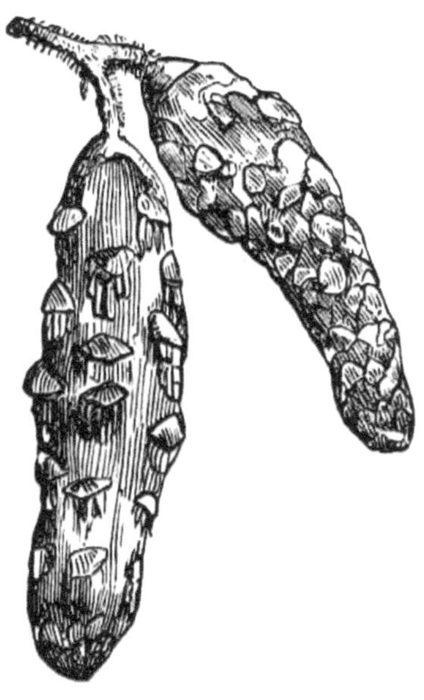

figure, in one of the tassels the flowers are fully open, and in the other they are not. Sometimes they are very delicate. They are in the black alder. It is curious to see how different they look when the flowers are open and when they are not. When they are open, they look beautiful, as seen through a microscope. When the chestnut-trees are in blossom, their tassels, hanging in clusters, give them a very rich appearance.

You have seen in this chapter that the variety of shapes in flowers is very great. It is almost without limit. Now the Creator makes all this variety of form for the same reason that he gives to flowers such a variety of colors. It is to feast our eyes and make us happy.

Questions.—*Mention* some of the shapes of flowers spoken of in the first of the chapter. Tell about the pea-blossom. Mention some flowers that are shaped like bells. Mention some that are cup-shaped. Mention some that are shaped like a tunnel. Tell about the calceolaria. Tell about the Indian turnip and the calla. What is said of the trumpet-creeper? Of the snap-dragon? Of the golden rod? What are compound flowers? Mention some of them. Tell about the white daisy. Also the mountain daisy. Mention some trees that have their flowers in tassels. Tell about these tassels. Why has God given such variety of shape to flowers?

CHAPTER VII.

HABITS OF FLOWERS.

FLOWERS HAVE habits, or ways of acting, just as people do. I will tell you about some of them.

All flowers naturally turn toward the light, as if they loved it. You can see this if you watch plants that are standing near a window. The flowers will all be bent toward the light if you let the pots stand just in the same way all the time. By turning the pots a little every day or two while the blossoms are opening, you can make the flowers look in different directions.

There are some flowers that shut themselves up at night as if to go to sleep, and open again in the morning. Tulips do this. I was once admiring in the morning some flowers that were sent to me the evening before by a lady. Among them were some tulips, and out of one of these, as it opened, flew a bumble-bee. A lazy, dronish bee he must have been to be caught in this way as the flower was closing itself for the night. Or, perhaps he had done a hard day's work in gathering honey, and just at night was so sleepy that he stayed too long in the tulip, and so was shut in. A very elegant bed the old bee had that night. I wonder if he slept any better than he would have done if he had been in his homely nest.

The pond-lily closes its pure white leaves at night as it lies upon its watery bed. But it unfolds them again in the morning. How beautiful it looks as it is spread out upon the water in the sunlight! The little mountain daisy that I told you about in the last chapter, is among the flowers that close at night. But it is as bright as ever on its "slender stem" when it wakes up in the morning. When it shuts itself up it is a little round green ball, and looks something like a pea. You would not see it in the midst of the grass if you did not look for it. But look the next morning, and the ball is opened, and shows "a golden tuft within a silver crown." And very beautiful it is when there are so many of the daisies together that the grass is spangled with them in the bright sun. It is supposed that this flower was at first called "day's eye," because it opens its eye at the day's dawn, and after a while it became shortened to daisy.

The golden flowers of the dandelion are shut up every night. They are folded up so closely in their green coverings, that they look like buds that have never yet been opened. The blossoms of the salsify, or vegetable oyster, close in the same manner, but not at the same time. They close always at noon. In the morning their tall, straight stalks make quite a brilliant appearance, each one having a deep purple flower at its top. All these are shut up in the afternoon, and you see at the top of each stalk a large pointed bud. The flowers of this plant are very much like the dandelion, both when closed and when open. The seeds, also, are very similar, as you will see in another chapter, and make together, around the top of the stalk, a similar feathery globe.

There is one curious habit which the dandelion has. When the sun is very hot it closes itself up to keep from wilting. It is in this way sheltered in its green covering from the sun. It sometimes, when the weather is very hot, shuts itself up as early as nine o'clock in the morning.

Some flowers hang down their heads at night as if they

were nodding in their sleep. But in the morning they lift them up again to welcome the light.

Some flowers have a particular time to open. The evening primrose does not open till evening, and hence comes its name. The flower called *four o'clock* opens at that hour in the afternoon. There is a flower commonly called *go-to-bed-at-noon*, that always opens in the morning and shuts up at noon.

Most flowers last for some time. But there are some that last only a few hours. The red flowers of the delicate and rich cypress-vine open in the morning, and in the afternoon they close up, never to open again. But there are always some buds to open every day. It is delightful to one who loves flowers to see every morning a new set of these bright blossoms appear among the fine dark-green leaves of this vine.

Questions.—*What* is said of flowers turning to the light? What do some flowers do at night? Tell about the bumble-bee. What is said of the pond-lily? What of the mountain daisy? What of the dandelion? What is said of the time of opening of some flowers? Tell about the flowers of the cypress-vine.

CHAPTER VIII.

MORE ABOUT THE HABITS OF FLOWERS.

YOU HAVE often seen the flowers of the morning-glory. These last only from early in the morning to noon, or a little after noon. In the afternoon they are all closed, and the vines look very dull without any flowers on them. But look the next morning, and you will see a plenty of these beautiful flowers. They open before most people are out of their beds. And, just as I told you about the cypress-vine, there is a new set of them every day.

It is curious to see in what way the blossom of the morning-glory opens and then shuts itself up to die. If you look in the afternoon you will find here and there a bud shaped as you see in this figure. The flower part of it, you observe, is twisted at its pointed end in a spiral manner; that is, something like a cork-screw. This bud will be an open flower the next morning.

On the following page you see the flower as it looks when it is fully opened. There are ribs running up from the lower part of the flower. Each of these ribs comes to a point at the edge. They give firmness to the blossom. They are its frame-work, its timbers. Without these ribs it could not stand like a cup on its stem, as it does now, but would hang loosely down. The open spread part of the flower is very thin, and the ribs are to it what the whalebones are to an umbrella.

In this figure you see how the flower

looks as it is partly closed. The points of the ribs are all turned in toward the middle of the flower. They bend in more and more, and after a while the flower wilts and dies. Now it is curious that the ribs of the flower should be folded so differently when it closes from what they are before it opens. Before it opens they are folded in a spiral form, as you see in the figure in the preceding page. When it closes, we would suppose that they would fold up in the same form. But they do not. They bend straight over, and the points come together in the middle of the flower.

There are some flowers that open only at night. That splendid flower, the night-blooming cereus, is one of them. And it opens only once. It lets us see its beauty only a few hours, and then it wilts and dies. It is a very large flower, and its opening is commonly watched for with great eagerness. It is a rare flower, and it is only now and then that we can get an opportunity of seeing it. It is very fragrant. It opens commonly quite late in the evening, and shuts itself up the latter part of the night. It never lets the light of day into its bosom. It makes us feel almost sad that so beautiful a flower lasts so short a time. We should feel really sad if most flowers did not last longer than this.

Through spring, summer, and autumn, we have a succession of flowers of every kind. Some last but a little while, and some feast our eyes for a long time. They come one after another. Each has its own season, and opens at its appointed time every year. In this succession of flowers we are never without some of them before us till the cold weather of winter comes again. God has thus kindly provided us with beautiful things to look upon, in the garden and in the field, through all the warmer months of the year.

In the spring the flowers are small and delicate, but are generally quite fragrant. In the summer we have very many more flowers than in spring or autumn. They have every variety of color and shape. They are commonly very fragrant, so that the air is filled with pleasant odors. In autumn the flowers generally have bright colors, and are very showy; but few of them have any fragrance.

Questions.—*How* are the flowers of the morning-glory like those of the cypress-vine? Tell about the bud of the morning-glory; also about the flower when it is open, its shape, and its ribs; also about the way in which it shuts up. What is said of the night-blooming cereus? Tell about the succession of flowers. How are the flowers of the spring, and summer, and autumn different?

CHAPTER IX.
WHAT LIVE ON FLOWERS.

FLOWERS ARE made chiefly for us to look at. It is to gratify our eyes, as I have before told you, that the Creator has made them so beautiful, and has given to them such a variety of shape and color. But they are good for something else besides this. Many different animals get their food from them. These animals are very small, and need but little food; but that little they get from flowers.

You see many different kinds of insects about most flowers. Most of these insects, we suppose, live upon the honey that they find there. We know that some do, for we see them gathering it. We see the bees do this. The busy little honey-bee goes from flower to flower, and gets a little honey from each. When he has gathered as much as he well can carry, off he flies to lay it up in the hive. A great many bees there are in one hive; and each bringing continually his little load, they after a while lay up a large amount of honey.

The bumble-bee, too, is busy among the flowers. See how quickly he flies from one flower to another, humming as he goes. Now he comes to a little flower, sticks his head in, and in a moment is off—buzz, buzz—for another. And now you see him come to a large, deep flower; and in he goes, almost out of sight, and his buzzing is stopped for some time. Soon he backs out to fly to another. And so he goes from flower to flower to gather his load of honey.

I have been amused to see how the bumble-bee manages with some flowers. The flower of the cypress-vine is very deep, but it is so small that he can not get into it so as to reach the honey. He knows that there is honey there, for he smells it. Now how do you think he gets at it? By working away a little while he pushes himself into the flower so as to split it open. And now he can come to the bottom of the flower where the honey is. In this way he spoils a great many flowers in getting his load of honey.

I have observed one thing about the bumble-bees that I do not understand. Some of them go inside of flowers to get their honey, while others go only on the outside, just at the bottom of the cup of the flower. It is curious to see two bumble-bees on one stalk of flowers, one going into all of them, and the other getting his honey from the outside of them. I have often seen this, but never could find the reason of it.

Another thing I have observed about the bumble-bees. Each one generally goes only to flowers of one kind. If, for instance, he begins with china-asters, he will go to no other flowers to gather his honey. He will sometimes take a look at others as he goes buzzing along, but he flies on till he finds some more china-asters. Soon off he starts for his nest, and perhaps, when he comes again, he goes to some other kind of flowers. If he begin now with morning-glories, you will see him pushing himself into every one that he comes to, and he will not stop at any other flower.

We commonly speak of the bees as gathering honey. This is not exactly correct. They *make* honey out of what they get from the flowers. And it is well known that the honey-bees, as they are called, can manufacture better honey from what they gather from some flowers than they can from what they gather from others. From the fragrant flowers of the garden and the white clover of the fields is made the deli-

cate white honey that you often see on the tea-table. But the bee can not always find such nice food; and then it flies off to the buckwheat fields, or perhaps helps itself to the drainings of some molasses or sugar cask in front of the grocer's door. Honey made from these things does very well for the bees' winter store, but it does not suit our taste.

Those beautiful insects, the butterflies, get their living among the flowers. As they fly about, they now and then stop and rest upon some flower, as you see this one doing. This is done not merely for the sake of resting, but to take some food from the flower.

Questions.—*What* use have flowers besides being beautiful to look at? What is said of the honey-bee? What of the bumble-bee? Tell how he manages with the flowers of the cypress-vine. What is said about bumble-bees going some to the inside and some to the outside of flowers? What is said about the making of honey? Tell about the butterflies.

CHAPTER X.
MORE ABOUT WHAT LIVE ON FLOWERS.

THE HUMMING-BIRD also lives on the flowers. This little creature seems always to be on the wing when he is not in his nest. He is seldom seen sitting on a branch like other birds. As he puts his long bill into a flower he does not stand on any thing. He is held up by his fluttering wings. His wings never seem to be still, but are always quivering. And then how very quickly he goes from one flower to another. He seems to dart as if by a sudden spring, instead of flying like other birds.

Here is a representation of a humming-bird, with his nest. It is the smallest nest that is made by a bird. It is nicely made. It is very soft inside with down and other things. The outside is generally covered with moss gathered from trees or fences. Fastened to the branch of a tree, as you see, it does not appear like a nest if you look at it sideways. It is so nearly of the same color with the bark of the branch,

that you would not be apt to observe it unless you were looking very sharply.

A lady once found a humming-bird that seemed almost dead. Its long slender tongue lay out of its bill, and it was very dry. She pitied the poor bird, and moistened its tongue with a little sugar and water. It drew its tongue in, and then put it out again. As it seemed to like the sugar and water, she gave it more. Soon the little creature was so revived that it was on its fluttering wings again, and flew off to sip something better than sugar and water from the beautiful flowers.

I have told you about the bees and butterflies. There are other insects besides these that seem to get their living from flowers. There is a great variety of them about flowers, if we look for them. St. Pierre, a Frenchman in Paris, watched a strawberry-plant that he had in a flower-pot. In three weeks he counted thirty-seven different kinds of insects that visited it.

If you go out into the garden in the middle of the day, you will see what a variety of insects there is. There are more about some flowers than about others. About some of them there are so many that it makes a very lively, busy scene. Besides the bees you will see flies of every color and of every size. Some are flying from flower to flower. Some seem to be on the wing all the time. These are all the while singing as they hover over the flowers, as if they enjoyed themselves very much in looking at such beautiful things. And others are resting themselves here and there, or are walking leisurely about.

Besides the flies, there are bugs crawling about on the flowers. These are of various sizes, and some of them are very small. Some of them have brilliant and rich colors.

There is a great deal of hum and stir about a plant where there are so many insects. It is just as it is where there are many people together. And as some people make more noise than others, so it is with insects. So, too, some insects are more bustling than others.

At night the scene is changed. The buzzing of the bees and the singing of the flies are done. The insects have got through with their work and their play, and have gone to the places where they sleep. If you look just at dusk at a plant that you have seen all alive with insects in the day, you will find all quiet. The insects are all gone, except, perhaps, some little ones that have gone into the flowers to sleep on the soft and elegant bed they find there.

Sometimes insects, like people, get into trouble by staying out late at night. On a cool morning I found a bumble-bee clinging to a flower. He was very torpid, and he could not fly when I poked him with a little stick. He could only buzz and thrust out his sting. After the sun warmed him he flew off. I suppose that he stayed out so late that he got chilled, and could not make his way home to his nest.

Questions.—*Tell* about the humming-bird, and about his nest. Give the anecdote told about a humming-bird. Tell about the Frenchman and his strawberry-plant. What is said of the variety of flies that we see about flowers? And of the variety of bugs? What is said of the hum and stir about some plants? How is it at night? Tell about the bumble-bee.

CHAPTER XI.
WHAT THE BIBLE SAYS ABOUT FLOWERS.

FLOWERS ARE often mentioned in the Bible. Man is said to be like a flower, because as he dies and is buried in the earth, so the flower fades and withers, and falls to the ground. I might give you many texts where this comparison is made. But I will mention only one, which you will find in the first chapter of the First Epistle of Peter, in the twenty-fourth verse. "For all flesh is as grass, and all the glory of man as the flower of grass. The grass withereth, and the flower thereof falleth away."

Man is compared in the Bible to a flower for another reason. Flowers live but a little while. This is true even of those that live the longest. Some last but a few hours, as I told you about the flowers of the morning-glory and the cypress-vine. So it is with mankind. Some die very young. These are like the morning-glories. They are beautiful while they live, and parents and friends like to look at them, just as we like to look at the beautiful flowers. But their life is short, very short, like a flower that blooms only for a day, and then withers and falls. When such a child dies, how appropriate to put flowers into the coffin! The dead child is beautiful and pleasant to look upon, like the flower cut from its stalk, and both will decay together.

But perhaps you will say that old persons are not like flowers, for they live a great while. It may seem a long time to you, but if you ask them, they will tell you that life, as they look back upon it, is very short. They are like the flowers that live the longest. While the infant that dies is like the flower that lives but a few hours, those that die old are like the flowers that last many days. That is all the difference. All flowers die, and so do all people, and other flowers and other people take their places.

In comparing people to flowers, the Bible speaks of them as being *cut down*. And you have perhaps seen in an old primer Time represented as an old man having a scythe, and underneath it reads:

> Time cuts down all,
> Both great and small.

It is because death is often so sudden both to young and old that they are said to be cut down like the grass or the flower. You see a beautiful flower standing among the grass, fresh and gay, in the bright sun. But the mower's scythe cuts it down, and it wilts and dies. So it is when death comes, as it sometimes does, to the strong and beautiful. So sudden is the change, that it seems as if they were really cut down like the flower.

There is one comparison about the beauty of flowers that you have often read in the Bible. It is this: "Consider the lilies of the field, how they grow; they toil not, neither do they spin; and yet I say unto you, that even Solomon in all his glory was not arrayed like one of these." Now Solomon had very rich clothing, for he was a very rich king. But take the richest clothing and look at it carefully, and then look at even common flowers, and you will say that they are much more beautiful than the clothing. And the difference is very great when you use a microscope. The splendid cloth looks coarse and rough when magnified. But it is not so with the flowers. The more they are magnified the more beautiful they appear.

Even flowers that we commonly think of as weeds, are beautiful when we come to examine them. The ox-eyed daisy is not considered at all pretty. But pick it and look at it carefully, and you will see much beauty in it. And if, with a microscope, you look at one of the six hundred flowers in its yellow bosom, you will say that in this weedy-looking flower there is a whole garden of beauties. Few people think much about the tassels that hang on so many of the trees and shrubs in the spring; but, as I have told you before, they are rich in beauty when we examine them.

Questions.—*Why* does the Bible compare man to a flower? What other reason is there for this comparison? What flowers are they like that die young, and what are they like that die old? Why are people when they die said to be cut down like the grass or the flower? What does the Bible say of the lilies of the field? What is the difference between cloth and flowers when you look at them carefully? What is the difference when you look at them through a microscope? What is said of the beauty of common and weedy-looking flowers?

CHAPTER XII.

WHEN A flower wilts and falls, there is something left on the end of the flower-stem. It is this that holds the seeds. You can see this in the rose. When the beautiful leaves of the flower are all scattered by the wind, there is a roundish thick part left on the end of the stem. The seeds are in this. It grows larger, and becomes of a reddish color. If you break it open you can see the seeds in it.

Here is represented this seed-holder of the rose, in the first figure as whole, and in the second as cut open to show the seeds. You see that the seeds crowd it full. There is no room for any thing else.

Now this we do not call fruit; for there is very little of it, and it does not taste good. But look at what is left when a pear-blossom falls. It is shaped very much like what is

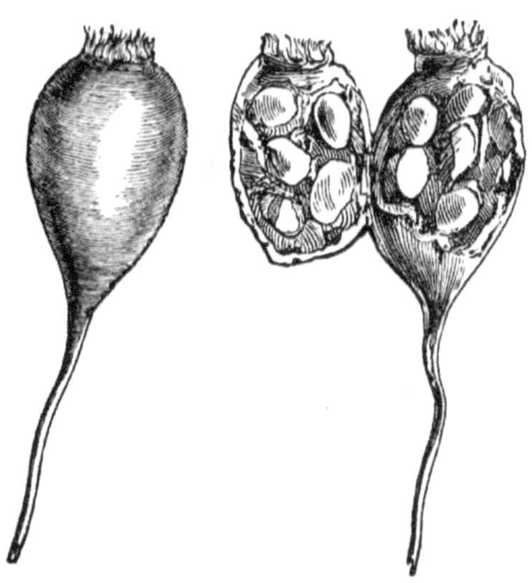

left when the leaves of the rose are scattered. But it grows more than that does. When it is fully grown it is larger than it need to be to hold the seeds. The seeds are but a small part of it. It is made to be eaten as well as to hold the seeds. So we call it fruit.

Here is a small pear

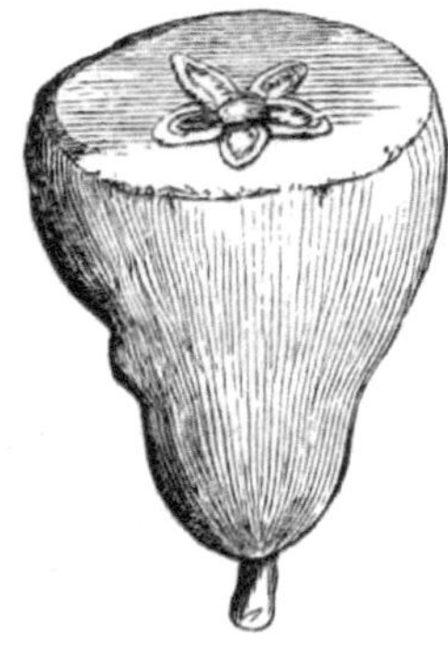

cut in such a way as to show the seeds. You see that it is very different from the pear-shaped seed-holder of the rose.

When the blossom of the orange falls, you see a little round green ball standing on the end of the stem. This grows very much, and when it is ripe it is large and of a yellow color. Just as it is with the pear, the orange is larger than it needs to be to hold the seeds. We call it fruit, because it is made for us to eat.

The little yellow flower of the currant, when it falls,

leaves a small, round berry. This grows, and becomes red when it ripens. So it is with the gooseberry. The whortleberry, you know, grows dark when it ripens. These berries have the seeds inside of them. The strawberry has its seeds on the outside, as you see here, and they give it a very pretty appearance.

These berries are all larger than they need to be to hold the seeds. The Creator intends them for fruit. But he never intended that what holds the rose-seeds should be fruit, and so he made it only large enough to hold the seeds.

The flowers on the grape-vine are very small and delicate. They are much smaller than the fruit that forms after they fall. The delicious grape is something more than a seed-holder. If it were meant only to hold the seeds, it would not have all that juicy pulp that is so pleasant to the taste.

Fruits are of very different sizes. The fruits of some vines are very large, as the pumpkin and the watermelon.

The fruits of some large trees are quite small. This is the case with the walnut and the chestnut. The acorn is a very small nut, but every child has been taught that
"Tall oaks from little acorns grow."
Some of the trees in warm climates bear very large fruit. Cocoa-nuts are an example.

The fruits of the earth that are most largely used by man are in the form of seeds. This is the case with grain, corn, peas, beans, etc. Most of what we raise of these is used for food, and we keep but a very small part for seed for the next year. The different kinds of grain and corn are used in making bread; and this, you know, is a part of our food that we depend upon so much, that it is called the staff of life. And this is the reason that in the Lord's Prayer bread is used as meaning food, when we say, Give us this day our daily bread.

The grains from which our bread is made are quite small. But there are a great many of them. And they are freed from their chaffy coverings, and are ground between mill-stones, so as to be changed into the fine flour, from which we make bread.

Questions.—*What* is said of the seed-vessel of the rose? How is a pear different from this? What is said of the orange? What of currants, strawberries, etc.? What is said of grapes? What is said of the different sizes of fruits? In what shape are the fruits that are most used by man? Why is bread called the staff of life? How do we get the flour from which we make bread?

CHAPTER XIII.

MORE ABOUT FRUITS.

YOU WILL want to know from what all the fruits are made. They are made from the sap, just as the flower is. After the flower has fallen the sap keeps coming along the pipes in the stem. And what is on the end of the stem is made from the sap into fruit.

You remember that I told you that a flower is never like the sap from which it is made. The same is true of the fruit. Bite the stem of a cluster of grapes, and you will see that the sap in it has none of the sweetness of the grapes; and yet they are made from it, just as the flowers were before them.

How different the fruit often is from the flower that was before it, though they are both made from the same sap! It may not, perhaps, seem strange to you that the sweet orange and its fragrant blossom can be made of the same sap; for, though they have different colors, they are both sweet. But how different a sour apple is from the blossom that was before it! And then, too, the orange was sour till it became ripe. But the sap constantly came to it through the stem, and the juice after a while became sweet. And see how different a thing the peel is from the pulp of the orange. It tastes quite sharp, and is sometimes bitter. But both peel and pulp are made from the same sap. So, too, the skin of some grapes has a very different taste from the pulp.

You see that there is a great variety in the fruits that God has given to us. I have said something before of their variety of size. They differ also in their taste, and color, and shape.

Some fruits are sour, and some are sweet. Many fruits have a taste that is very different from the taste of any other fruit, and yet you can not describe it. The chestnut does not taste like the walnut, but you can not describe the difference to any one so that he would know it. He must taste them himself to know the difference. Grapes and whortleberries are both sweet, but they do not taste alike. There is a great variety of sour apples, but you always readily see the difference between them when you eat them.

There is a great variety in the *colors* of fruits. But it is not as great as the variety of color in flowers. The Creator made flowers especially to please the eye. It is for this that he has given them many different colors. He could have made fruits without having any flowers. But he, in his kindness, wished to have us gratified by looking at beautiful things.

Flowers are for beauty, and fruits for use. But many of the fruits are beautiful. Our heavenly Father likes to make beauty go along with what is useful. The orange has a rich color, and looks beautiful among the green leaves. We admire the clusters of grapes, as they hang by their slender stems under the broad leaves of the vine. The colors of some of the varieties of the peach and the apple are very rich. The strawberry looks very beautiful, as the yellow seeds stand out on its red surface.

There is a great variety in the *forms* of fruits. Look at the chestnut burr, and see how different it is from a fair-skinned, round apple. How different is the strawberry that melts in your mouth from any of the hard nuts! How different is the cocoa-nut from a melon!

God smiles upon us in the flowers. But in the fruits we

have something more than his smiles. In them he blesses us with his bounty. The flowers are a feast to our eyes; but the fruits are food to our bodies.

But fruits are not made merely to nourish us. They are so made that they gratify our taste while they nourish us and sustain our lives. And in this we see the kindness of our heavenly Father, just as we do in the beauty that he has given us to look upon in both flowers and fruits. He could have made the fruits in such a way that they would be without any pleasant taste. And they would have answered as well to nourish us as they now do. But he wanted to gratify us in this as he does in other things. For this purpose he has given to each kind of fruit its own taste. All fruits are pleasant, but each is different from the rest.

The variety of pleasant tastes in the fruits of the earth is very great, as you will see if you will think of as many of them as you can. What an evidence is this of God's abundant goodness! He does not gratify us merely in a few things, but in many things. The pleasant things of this world are almost endless in their variety. How strange it is that any one can know all this, and live on day after day without any gratitude to his Maker!

Questions.—*What* are fruits made from? Is the fruit ever like the sap? What is said about the orange? What is said of the taste of fruits? What of their colors? What of their different forms? What is it said that God does in the flowers, and what in the fruits? Why is there such a variety of pleasant tastes in fruits?

CHAPTER XIV.
WHAT SEEDS ARE FOR.

IN TELLING you about fruits I told you also something about seeds. In this chapter I shall tell you more about them. Plants commonly come up from seeds. It is very curious to see how this is done. But most people do not think much about it. Gardeners and farmers put seeds into the ground. They see the plants come up from them. They see these plants grow and blossom, and after a while they gather fruit from them. And they do not seem to think that there is any thing wonderful in all this. But when you have read what I shall tell you about it, I think that you will say that it is very wonderful.

You put a bean into the ground. A vine comes up from it. This runs up a pole, winding round and round it as it goes up. It blossoms. Then come the pods. In these are beans just like that which you put into the ground. All this comes from that single little bean. And there is nothing there like what you put into the ground but the beans. The vine, the leaves, the flowers, are nothing like the bean from which they grew.

When you put a kernel of corn in the ground there comes up a stalk. From this spread out broad, long leaves. At length large ears of corn form. A great deal has come from that single kernel. And of all this only the kernels of corn on the ear are like what you put into the ground.

An acorn falls from an oak-tree. This is the seed. But nothing will grow from it unless it gets into the ground. A cow perhaps treads on it, and so presses it into the earth.

A twig shoots up from it. This, after many years, grows to be a large tree. Here a very great deal has come from the seed in the ground. And the huge tree is not at all like the little acorn from which it came.

You will want to know how it is that so much comes from a small seed. I will now tell you as much about this as I can.

After a seed has been in the ground a little while it swells, because the dampness of the earth gets into it. The covering of the seed breaks, and out comes a little root. This root pushes down into the ground. Pretty soon there comes out of the seed also a little stalk. This shoots upward. Here is a representation of a seed which has burst. And you see the root, with its fine fibres, going down while the stalk goes up. Now what makes the root go down and the stalk go up we do not know. Many very wise men have tried to find this out. But they can not do it. They have guessed a good deal about it; but guessing is not knowing, though people often think it is. The Creator knows, and he makes the root of every seed go down and the stalk go up. There is never any mistake about this. You never see a root pushing up through the ground and a stalk growing down.

Here you see the way in which a barley-seed grows. Roots branch out from one end of the seed down into the ground, and a stalk goes up from the other end of it. It is

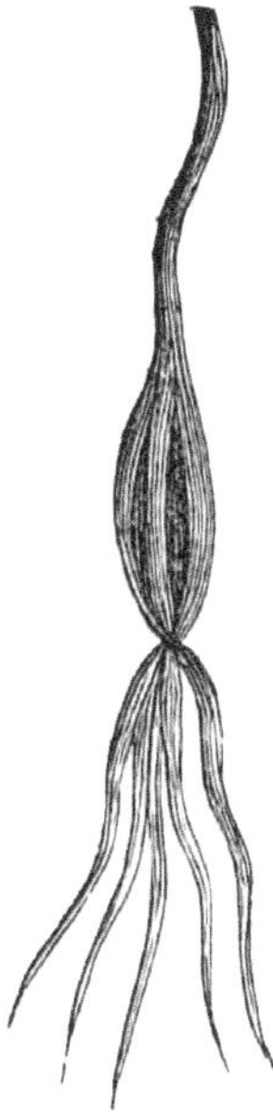

so also with corn. No matter how the seed lies in the ground, the roots will go down, even if they come out of the upper end of the seed; and the stalk will go up to find the air, though it must first come out of the lower end.

Roots sometimes seem to take a great deal of pains, as we may say, to get down into the ground. A seed of a tree was seen to take root, in Galloway in Scotland, on an old stone wall ten feet from the ground. And a tree shot up from it. There was earth enough in the crevices of the wall to make the little tree grow for a while. But after a time it stopped growing. The reason was that the tree had become so large that it could not get food enough out of the earth in the wall. The little mouths in the root sucked up all they could find; but it was not enough. The tree needed more food than when it was small, just as a man needs more food than an infant. What was to be done? There was a plenty of food in the ground below, but the trouble was to get at it. If somebody would take the tree from the wall, and set it down into the ground, it would do well enough. But no one did this. So the tree managed the matter itself. It sent its roots down the wall the whole ten feet into the ground. And then it grew finely, and would have done well if the wind had not blown it over. It was so stilted up on the wall that it could not stand against a strong wind as a tree could whose roots spread right from the bottom of its trunk into the ground.

I have mentioned the covering of the seed. If you look at a bean you will see that it has a firm skin. This bursts open for the root and the stalk to come out. The place where it bursts is what is called the eye. The potato, you know, has many eyes. When it is put into the ground a root and a stalk will come out from each one of them. You sometimes see potatoes sprout from the eye as they lie in the cellar.

There is great difference in the coverings of different seeds. The covering of some nuts is very hard. You see this in the peach-stone, the walnut, and the cocoa-nut. How do you think these are opened so that the root and stalk may push out? I will tell you. The peach-stone and the walnut, by being soaked in the ground, swell and crack open. And as to the cocoa-nuts, it is said that the monkeys crack them open by throwing them on the ground. So it is in various ways that the prison-house of the seed, as we may call it, is opened.

Questions.—What come from seeds? Do most people think that there is any thing wonderful in this? Tell what comes from a single bean. What from a kernel of corn. What from an acorn. How does the seed begin to grow? What is said about the stalks shooting up and the roots going down? Tell about the barley-seed. What is told about a tree? What is the eye of a seed? What is said about the difference in the coverings of seeds? How are some hard seeds opened, so that the root and stalk may push out?

CHAPTER XV.
LIFE IN THE SEED.

A DRY seed looks as if it were dead. But there is life there, shut up in that prison-house. It is very quiet as long as it is shut up. But once let it out, and it does great things. An apple-seed, with its stout brown covering, is a very little thing. It does not look as if any thing could ever come from it. But if it gets into the ground, the moisture swells it, the covering bursts, and an apple-tree comes from the seed. And you know the Bible tells us, a tree large enough for the fowls of the air to lodge in its branches comes from the little mustard-seed.

The life in the dry seed is asleep. Put it into the moist ground, and this life wakes up. This sleep of seeds sometimes lasts a great while. Commonly we keep them only from one year to another. But sometimes they are kept a long time in their state of sleep. I will tell you a story about this: Many hundred years ago there came a great stream of lava, as it is called, down from a mountain. It was all on fire, and looked like a stream of melted iron. It rolled over a city and covered it up. All the inhabitants were killed. When the lava cooled, people came to look for the city, but could not find any of it. But lately, people have dug down through the lava, and opened passages into this covered-up city. They have gone into the houses, and have found many things just as they were when the red-hot lava ran over the city. Some seeds were found. These were planted; and they sprung up just as seeds do that have been kept only from one year to another. The life in these seeds, then, had been asleep for many hundred years.

A great many seeds come from one seed put into the ground. From a single kernel of corn come several ears full of kernels. The kernels or seeds from one single ear are enough to plant quite a large piece of ground. We use most of the corn for food, for we need to keep but little of it for seed. So we eat most of the beans that we raise. We keep only a little bag of them for planting the next year. As you look at the little bag, you would hardly think that it holds what will cover long rows of poles with vines. There is a great deal of life asleep for the winter in that bag.

Most of the seeds that drop from trees and plants are killed, and they decay on the ground with the leaves. It is only now and then that a seed lives and takes root. If all seeds lived and sprung up we should have too many things growing every where. If all the acorns lived, and got into the ground, and took root, there would be too many oaks. And so of other trees and plants. The seeds that are scattered on the ground have to take their chance, as we say. Some out of the whole live through the winter in some way, and come up in the spring.

Questions.—What is said of life in the seed? What wakes it up? Can the sleep of seeds sometimes last a great while? Tell about the seeds from a city that was covered up with lava. What is said of the number of seeds that come from one seed? What becomes of the seeds of plants and trees that fall to the ground?

CHAPTER XVI.

HOW SEEDS ARE SCATTERED.

SEEDS ARE scattered in various ways. They do not all stay near the place where they drop.

There are many kinds of seeds that man scatters in raising his crops from year to year.

Some seeds are carried away by water. Sometimes they sail a very great distance in this way, and, like people, settle down far away from the spot where they grew.

Seeds are sometimes carried about in the hair of animals, and are dropped here and there. The sheep gets seeds into its wool, and then shakes them out as it goes about the pasture, or rubs them off against the trees and the fences. The little burrs with which you make baskets, by sticking them together, are seed-holders. They often stick to your clothes. When you pick them off and throw them away, you help to scatter seeds just as the sheep does.

The wind is the great scatterer of seeds. It blows them about if they are at all light. It sometimes takes them far away from where they grew. Some seeds are made in such a way that the wind can blow them about very easily. Look at the seed of the maple-tree. There is a sort of wing on it, as if it were made to fly. So when it falls, it goes whirling away in the air. It does not drop just by the tree if the air is stirring.

Here is a representation of two seeds of the maple, with their wings. They always grow in this way, in pairs.

Look at the little feathery ball on the stalk of the dandelion after the flower is gone. The seeds are in the middle

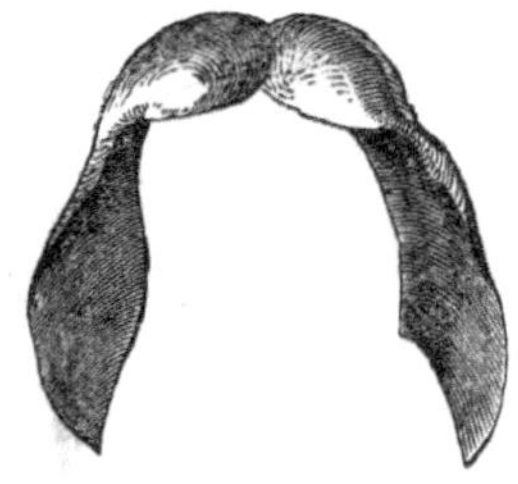

of that ball. Pick it, and then hold it up, and blow upon it as hard as you can. Away will fly all the seeds. If the wind is blowing it will scatter them every where. Now look at them to see what makes them fly so. You see that each seed has a very little stem. This stem has on its end some very fine fibres standing out all around. The wind blows the seed about by these fibres. If the seed did not have this sort of balloon to fly with, it would fall straight to the ground. But with this it may go a great distance. Sometimes it travels over mountains and across rivers. Here is a drawing of the dandelion-seed. But to see how delicate it is, and how well fitted it is to fly, you must look at a real seed.

And here is the stem of the dandelion as it looks after the seeds are scattered. You see that it has a cushion-shaped end. It is on this that the seeds are fastened. It is curious to see how regularly they are arranged so as to make that beautiful feathery ball.

The seed of the salsify represented here, is very much like that of the dandelion. But the fibres by which it is carried about by the wind are, you see, very delicately feathered.

The seed of the clematis or virgin's-bower is, as you see, rather differently arranged. It has a very long

stem, with little fibres standing out from it all the way, something like a feather.

The down of thistles and some other flowers is the wing of the seeds by which they are scattered by the wind. Here is a representation of a seed with its wing of down. This little seed has a very large wing to fly with.

The seeds of mosses and ferns are scattered more widely than any others because they are so small. You know the mosses well. You see them every where on fences, rocks, and trunks of trees, as well as on the ground. The wind carries their fine seeds about, and they lodge on every thing. They go even to the tops of the mountains, and down into caverns in the earth. There is great variety in the mosses, and some of them are exceedingly beautiful, especially when examined with a microscope.

Questions.—*In* what different ways are seeds scattered about? What is the great scatterer of seeds? What is said of the seeds of the maple? What of the seeds of the dandelion? What of the seeds of the salsify—the clematis—the thistle? What of the seeds of mosses and ferns?

CHAPTER XVII.

LEAVES.

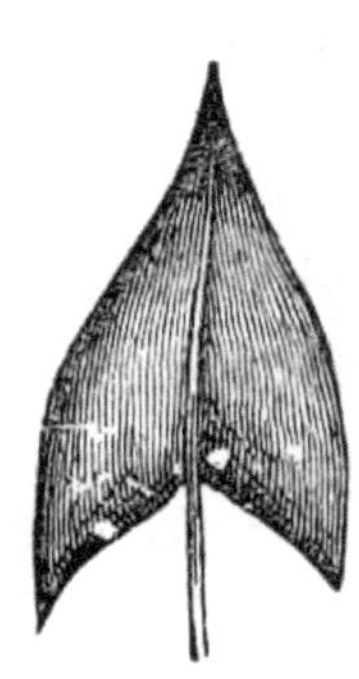

Most trees and bushes are stripped of all their leaves in the autumn, and remain bare till the winter is passed. We should feel sad if they were without leaves all the year round. One use of the leaves is to gratify us by their beauty. When the winter is gone how delightful it is to us to look out upon the trees and the plants as they put forth their leaves! Their fresh green color is a feast to our eyes.

You remember what I said about the flowers having so many different shapes. The Creator has made the same variety in the shapes of leaves. He likes to make beautiful things in great variety for us to look at. Here I give you some figures of leaves, to show you how different their shapes are.

Here is a leaf which is shaped like the head of an arrow. There is a plant called arrow-head, because its leaf has this shape.

Here is one shaped very much like a lance, another is a good representation of a mason's trowel, and a third is very much like a fiddle.

This is like a shield. The nasturtium the leaves of this kind. The stem is fastened to the leaf just where the hand holds on to a shield.

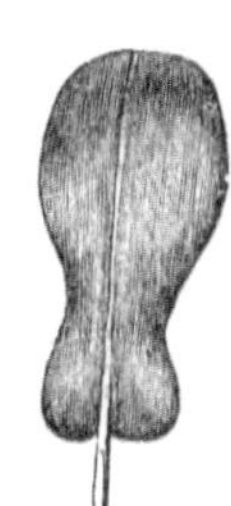

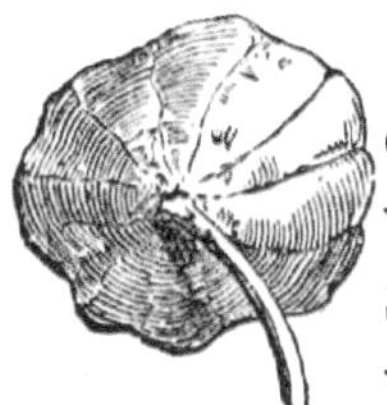

This leaf has a tendril on the end of it. This clasps around whatever it happens to touch. Some plants are held up in this way by their leaves.

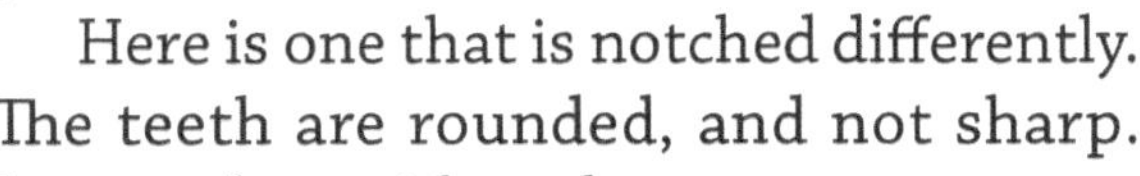

This leaf is notched all around its edge, like a saw. The leaves of a great many plants are notched in this way, as those of the rose, the peach, and the nettle.

Here is one that is notched differently. The teeth are rounded, and not sharp. It may be said to be scalloped rather than toothed. The ground ivy has a leaf of this kind.

Below are two leaves, one of which is spread out like a hand, and the other is very much like the claws of the feet of some birds. The passion-flower is of the shape of the hand. So, also, is that of the castor-oil plant.

I have thus given only a few of the shapes of leaves. Their variety is very great. They vary not only in shape, but in color. They vary also in other things. Some have down on

them, and some hairs, and some have neither. It will be well for you to see how many different kinds of leaves you can bring to the teacher, and she will tell you about them.

Leaves are arranged in a great many different ways on their stems. Here are three leaves together on a stem. The leaves of the clover and the wood-sorrel are arranged in this way.

Here the leaf-stem has three little branches, and each branch has three leaves.

On this leaf-stem are a great many leaves. I have thus shown you three ways in which leaves are arranged. But there are many other ways in which they are arranged, making a great variety in the appearance of leaves. The only way to know how very great this variety of arrangement is, is to look for yourselves at plants, and trees, and shrubs, as you walk in the garden or in the fields.

Leaves are of all sizes. Some are very small, and some are very large. Look at the little delicate leaves of the chickweed and the cypress-vine, and then at the large spreading leaves of the rhubarb-plant and the pumpkin-vine, and the very long ones of the corn. The common palm-leaf fans so much in use are made from the large leaves of the palm-tree.

I think that you will be quite interested in observing the various forms of leaves, though most people do not observe them much. A friend once told me that a number of leaves from our common trees were brought to some ladies, and that not one of them could tell from what kind of tree each leaf came. It seems to me that they could have used their eyes to little purpose, as they walked about among the trees of the field and the garden. They probably looked at leaves merely as making a pleasant green to the eye, and never examined them, as they perhaps would flowers, to see what a difference there is between them. You had better gather some leaves of various kinds, and see if your schoolmates can tell from what trees they came. Take the star-shaped leaf of the maple, the birch-leaf with its nicely notched edges, the bright, firm leaf of the oak with its wavy edge, and the wrinkled leaf of the elm. Show them a willow-leaf beside a peach-leaf, which is very much like it. An apple-leaf and a pear-leaf together might puzzle them, though I think that some wide-awake child would see the difference between them.

Questions.—*What* is said of one of the uses of leaves? What of the variety in their shapes? Mention some of these shapes. In what other things do leaves vary besides shape? What is said of the arrangement of leaves on their stems? What is said of their different sizes? What is said about observing the shapes of leaves?

CHAPTER XVIII.

MORE ABOUT LEAVES.

LEAVES ARE such common things that we do not think how beautiful they are. But take any common leaf into your hand and look at it. Take the leaf of the strawberry. See how prettily it is notched. Hold it up to the light and see the lines that run from the middle line to the edge. Then see the fine net-work between these lines. How delicate and beautiful! The leaf of the raspberry is even more beautiful than the strawberry leaf, if you pick it from a new shoot. See the fine points on its edge, and see how delicate are its lines and net-work as you hold it up to the light.

Observe the back of a leaf, and you will see ribs that spread out from the main rib in the middle to the edges. These are the frame of the leaf, just as timbers are the frame of a house. They are to the leaf what whalebones are to an umbrella. They give strength to it. Without them it would droop like a wilted leaf. It would not stand out straight and firm. The wind would blow it every way, like a rag tied to a stick.

You see these ribs very large in broad spreading leaves. They are large in grape-leaves, and in the leaves of the rhubarb-plant, or pie-plant, as it is often called.

In leaves that are very stiff and firm these ribs are so small, that at first you would say there were none. This is the case with the leaf of the pear and the orange. There is one strong rib running through in the middle of the leaf. But there are no strong ribs branching out from this. The leaf is so firm that it does not need them.

See the difference there is between the upper and the under side of a leaf. The upper is greener than the under side. In the grape-leaf the under side is covered with a very fine white fuzz. If you tear the leaf gently, you can see the delicate white fibres of this furze across the rent. In the silver-leaf poplar there is a silvery whiteness on the under side of the leaf. This makes the tree look very pretty as its branches are moved back and forth by the wind.

I have thus told you a few things about leaves. By looking at them yourselves you will see a great many things in them that will interest you. Look at them as you walk in the garden or roam in the field, and you will see that there is no end to the variety. And among them all you can not find one that is not beautiful when you examine it.

Leaves are very beautiful if you look at them through a microscope. Take the most common leaf and look at it in this way, and you will be delighted. You will be surprised to find how much beauty there is in leaves that you knew nothing about before.

And now I will tell you about some leaves of a very singular character.

There are some leaves that are of very singular shape. I will mention only a few.

Here is the leaf of the side-saddle flower, as it is called. It is shaped somewhat like a butter-boat. You see that it is open. It can hold considerable water. It has a kind of 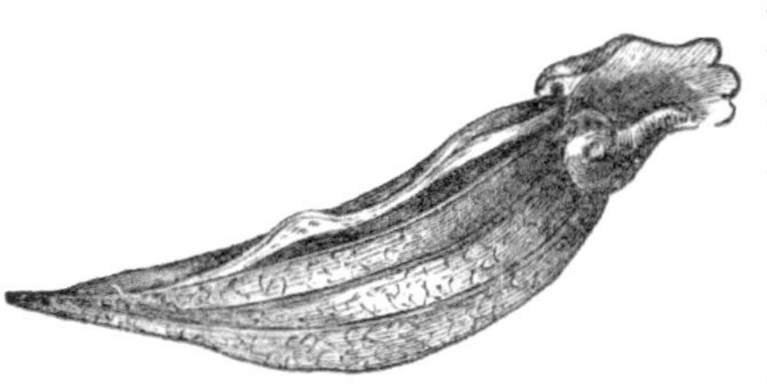 lip, which looks as if it were made in order that water might be poured out of it easily. This plant grows in some parts of this country. The flower is purple, and has a curious shape. It is on a stalk that stands up in the midst of about half-a-dozen of these leaves.

One of the most singular leaves is that of the Chinese pitcher-plant. At the end of the leaf the main rib extends out like a tendril, and this ends in the appendage which is represented here. It is in the shape of a pitcher, and has, as you see, a regular lid. This is generally shut down, though, as you see it here, it is raised up. The rain can not, therefore, get in, and yet the pitcher is always full of water. It holds about a tumblerful. Now how do you think this water comes there? It is a part of the sap that comes to the leaf. The watery part of the sap is poured from thousands and thousands of little mouths on the inside of the pitcher; and so it is kept filled with water. This plant is quite common in the island of Ceylon. There it is called monkey-cup, because the monkeys sometimes open the lid and drink the water. And men sometimes drink from these leaves when there is no spring of water where they can quench their thirst.

The leaf of the Venus's fly-trap, which grows in North Carolina, is a real trap for flies and other insects. Here you see the leaf as it is spread out, wide open. It looks as if there was no danger there. But let an insect alight on the leaf, and he is made a prisoner at once. The two parts of the leaf close

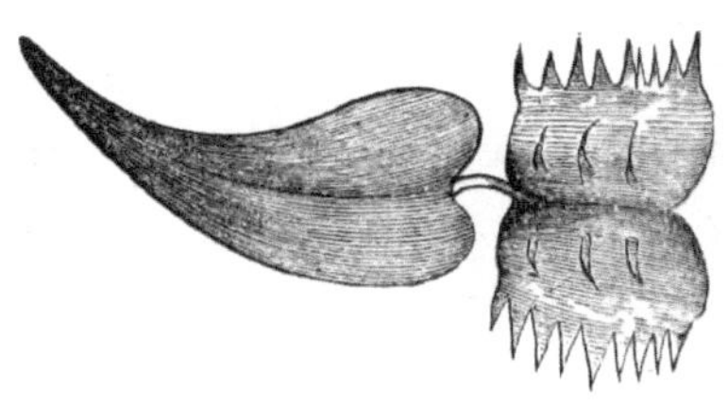

together, as you see, and the points on the edges are locked together, so as to furnish bars to the prison. You see a little insect caught in this leaf that had lighted only on its very edge. He can not get away, and there, poor fellow! he must die a slow death. Of what use it is to have such traps for insects we do not understand.

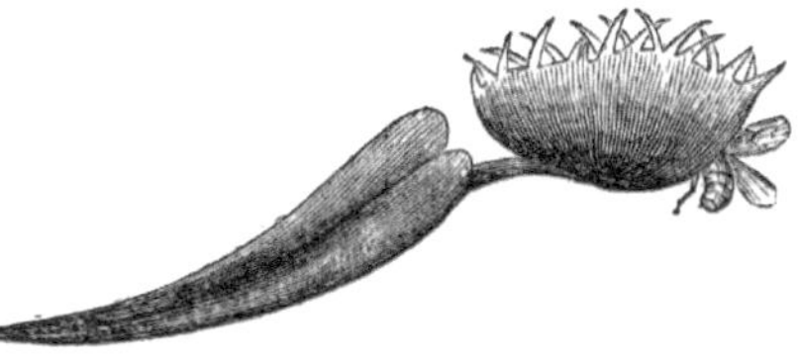

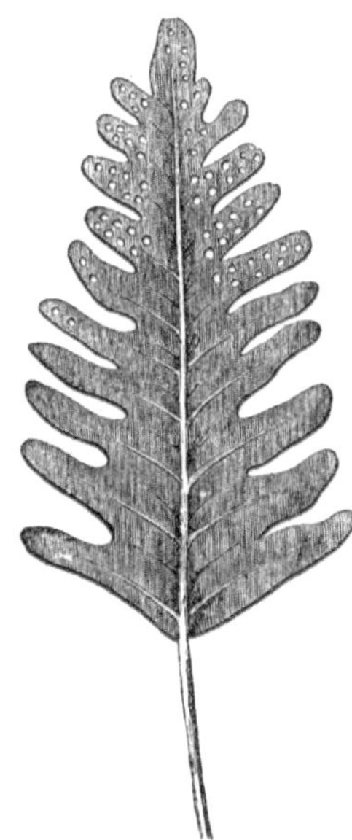

This is the leaf of the common fern or brake. It is beautiful if you examine it, for it is very delicate. And it has one great peculiarity. The flowers of the plant are on the under side of the leaf. They are where you see the little round spots. If you look at the leaf with a microscope you can see the different parts of the flowers.

Most leaves are thin, but some are quite thick. This is the case with the leaves of the India-rubber tree. The wax-plant has thick leaves, which, with the flowers, look so waxy as to give the name to the plant. The flowers of the cactuses grow right out from the thick fleshy leaves, making these plants look very awkward, although the flowers are so beautiful. And it is a singular fact, that if one of the leaves is broken off and put into the ground it will take root and grow.

Did you ever make a blow-bag, as it is called, of the leaf of the live-forever, as children very often do? If you have not, I will tell you how it is done. The leaf is rather thick, and is made of two layers. These you can separate at the stem-end of the leaf, and then by pinching the leaf and blowing into it you can make it puff out like a bag. You must do this very carefully, or you will break the layer on the under side of the leaf, which is very thin, while the upper layer is thick.

The leaf of the ribbon-grass, as it is called, is very singular in one respect. It is very prettily striped, but you can not find any two leaves that are striped exactly alike, any more than you can find two faces exactly alike among all the people on the earth.

Questions.—*What* is said of the beauty of common leaves? Tell about the ribs of leaves. What leaves have large ribs? How is it with the leaf of the pear and the orange? What is the difference between the upper and the under side of leaves? Tell about the grape-leaf. And about the leaf of the silver-poplar. What is said of the beauty of leaves as seen through the microscope? Tell about the leaf of the side-saddle flower. And about the Chinese pitcher-plant. Also about the Venus's fly-trap. What is said of the leaf of the common fern? What of thick leaves? What of the leaf of live-forever? What of ribbon-grass?

CHAPTER XIX.

THE SAP IN LEAVES.

I HAVE told you about the ribs of leaves. Let us see what makes them so firm and strong. Look at a large grape-leaf on the vine. It spreads out very firmly. If the wind blows it very hard it bends, but it stands out again as firmly as ever. But break the leaf off, and see what happens. In a little time it wilts. If you hold it up by the stem its edges droop down all around. The leaf does not stand out as it did when it was on the vine. The ribs are all there, but they have lost their strength. How do you think they lost it? I will tell you.

When you broke off the stem, the sap could no longer get to the leaf. It is just as no water can get into a house when the water-pipe is cut off outside. The sap goes to all parts of the leaf from the stem through the ribs. The ribs, like the stem, have little fine pipes in them for the sap to run in. Now, if the ribs are not full of the sap they are not firm, and they bend easily. When these ribs and the net-work between them are not full of sap the leaf is *wilted*, as we say.

But when the leaf is picked it is full of sap. How does any of the sap then get out of it so as to make it wilt? It does not leak out of the stem. If it did, you could see it drop as you hold the leaf up. Where, then, does it get out? This I will explain to you. There are little holes, or pores, as they are called, all over the leaf. They are so small that you can not see them without a strong microscope. The watery part of the sap escapes into the air through these pores.

There is a great deal of moisture that comes from leaves. You can see that this is so if you put a cluster of leaves under a glass vessel. A large tumbler will answer. You will, after a little time, see the moisture in drops on the inside of the glass. This moisture is the water that comes from the pores of the leaves.

You remember what I told you in the last chapter about the leaf of the pitcher-plant. The water in that leaf comes from its pores on the inside. If, instead of its having a pitcher-shape, the leaf was laid open and spread out like common leaves, the moisture would all go off in the air. But as it is a pitcher with a lid, the moisture that comes from all the pores is shut in. It can not fly off in the air. And after a while enough moisture collects to fill the pitcher. This shows how much water commonly goes from leaves into the air. If any leaf that you see spread out could be changed into a pitcher or cup shape with a lid, it would in a little time be full of the water that comes from its pores.

Now you can understand why a leaf wilts after it is picked. It does not wilt as soon as you pick it, for the sap is all in it then. But let it be a little while. The watery part of the sap is going out of the pores of the leaf all the time, and there is no sap coming to it through the stem. So the leaf wilts.

You can keep a leaf from wilting for a long time by placing the stem in water. When you do this the water goes up through the little pipes in the stem. This takes the place of the water that goes out of the pores of the leaf.

When you put flowers in water, you know that the water is less the next day. This is because so much of the water goes up in the stems to the leaves and blossoms.

You know that if you have a plant in a flower-pot, the

earth gets dry in a day or two. This is chiefly because the water in the earth is sucked up by the roots, and runs up all through the plant, and goes out of the pores of the leaves and blossoms. Some of the water goes up directly from the earth into the air, but most of it goes through the plant.

You can not see the water that comes out of the leaves and blossoms into the air. There is a great deal of water in the air that you can not see. You have often seen in a hot day the water stand in drops on the outside of your tumbler. Just think how these drops come there. People sometimes say that the tumbler sweats, just as if the water came through the glass. But this, you know, can not be. Water can not get through glass. The drops come there in this way. The cold water in the tumbler makes the glass very cold. And the water in the warm air around the tumbler, therefore, gathers upon it. Sometimes there is much more water in the air than there is at other times. Then the tumbler is very wet. Now a great deal of the water in the air comes from the leaves of the trees and the plants all about us. The leaves may be said to be breathing moisture into the air all the time. I shall tell you more about the water that is in the air in Part Third.

This moisture that is breathed out from the leaves makes the air soft, while the fragrance of the flowers makes it balmy. Each leaf yields but a little water, and so does but little good in this way. But there are so many leaves that a great deal of water comes from all of them. It puts me in mind of the Scotch proverb, "Many a little makes a mickle."

Those who want to do good in the world may learn a lesson from the leaves. A large amount of good may be done when a great many do each a little. Let those who can do but little think of this. Let them do every day what they can, just as each leaf does. Great men, that excite the wonder of the world, can do a great deal of good; but they can not do any thing like as much as is done by a great many people together that do each a little in a noiseless way. Every child, in doing little kind things, may, like the small leaf, do his part of the good that is to be done in the world. And if much of the good that he does is not noticed by others, God sees it all, just as he sees all the moisture that is breathed out by each little leaf.

Questions.—*What* makes the ribs of leaves firm? What happens to these ribs when a leaf wilts? How does the watery part of the sap get out of a picked leaf? What is said of the quantity of water that comes from leaves? Tell about the water in the leaf of the pitcher-plant. How does a picked leaf wilt? How does putting a leaf in water keep it from wilting? What makes the earth in a flower-pot become dry? Can you see the water that goes into the air from the leaves and other things? Tell about water settling on tumblers in hot weather. What lesson can we learn from the leaves?

CHAPTER XX.
THE USES OF LEAVES.

ONE USE of leaves, as I told you in the last chapter, is to supply the air with water. In the hot weather the air would be very dry and uncomfortable to us if the leaves did not breathe out moisture from their pores. You can see how this is if in a hot day you walk across a sandy plain where there are no leaves except those of the scanty grass and weeds. Here no moisture is breathed out upon you, to lessen the heat that you suffer from the burning sun.

Another use of the leaves is this. They are pleasant and beautiful to the sight. I have told you about this use of them in the beginning of the seventeenth chapter.

Another use of leaves is to give shade. We know how refreshing this is to us in a hot day. When in a city we walk through streets where there are no trees, how delightful it is to come out of the blazing sun into a square that is full of trees! How comfortable are the cows in the pasture lying under the trees at mid-day, chewing the cud!

But the shade given by leaves does good not merely to man and animals. It does good to fruits, if there is not too much of it. The sun would very often be too hot for the fruits, if it shone full on them all the time. So the leaves partly shade them.

The chief use of leaves is to keep plants and trees alive and make them grow. If you should strip off the leaves from a plant as fast as they came out, you would, after a while, kill it. Sometimes worms eat up the leaves on trees. If this is done year after year to a tree it dies. I knew a man to strip off all the leaves from a grape-vine. He thought that it would make the grapes grow finely. He had seen people take off some of the branches from grape-vines, to make the grapes grow large and full. So he thought that if he took *all* the leaves off, the sap would all go into the grapes and make them very large. He thought, too, that the sun would make them ripen fast. But he found that the grapes stopped growing, and wilted, and dropped off. There are two reasons for this. The sun was too hot for the grapes when all the leaves were gone. And besides, there were some leaves needed to keep the grapes alive.

Leaves are the same thing to plants that lungs are to an animal. The air that goes into our lungs helps to keep us alive and make us grow. So the air that is all about the leaves of a plant or tree helps to keep it alive and to make it grow. How this is done you can not understand now. I explain it in another book, which you will be able to understand when you are a little older.

There is one thing about this that you can understand, which is very curious. The air does not keep the plants alive in just the same way that it does animals. You know that by breathing air we make it bad; and so we must have all the time a supply of fresh air. Now what do you think becomes of the bad part of the air that we breathe out from the lungs? The leaves all around us take it in. It is good for them. It makes them and the plants that they are on grow. They then, like our lungs, are all the time taking in air and giving out air. And leaves take what lungs give, and lungs take what leaves give. So lungs and leaves have a sort of trade together. They are always making this exchange with each other. And it is a good bargain for both. Both get what they want, and barter away what they do not want.

But in winter, when the leaves are all gone except those on the evergreens, how is it with this trade between lungs and leaves? Lungs are all the time giving out bad air; but there are not leaves enough on the evergreens to take it all, and give back the good air. Well, what is to be done? A barter is carried on with the leaves a great way off in the southern countries. The air moves about so freely that this is easily done. The bad air goes there, and the leaves that take it into their pores give out the good air, which immediately spreads every where, even to us at the north. It is a free trade—as free as air, as we may say. There is not as much bad air made by lungs in winter as in summer, because many animals are either dead or torpid. But what is made is disposed of mostly in this way.

Questions.—How are leaves useful to us in giving out moisture to the air? What use of them is next mentioned? What is said of the shade made by leaves? Is this shade useful to fruits? What is the chief use of leaves? Tell about the man who stripped the leaves from his grape-vine. How are leaves like our lungs? What kind of barter is there between leaves and the lungs of animals? How is this barter carried on in winter?

CHAPTER XXI.

LEAVES IN THE AUTUMN.

IN THE autumn in cold climates the leaves fall. This is the reason that the autumn is called the fall of the year. There are some trees that have leaves on them all the time. These are called evergreens. In very hot climates the leaves of trees and bushes are out all the year round. They have no particular time to fall. And some leaves stay on for many years. Those that stay on so long grow to be very large.

If a tree or a bush that has its leaves fall in the autumn in a cold climate be raised in a warm climate, it will there keep its leaves on all the year. In the southern parts of Europe quince-trees are evergreen. The currant-bush, which, you know, with us is bare through the winter, in a hot country has leaves on it all the year.

Before the leaves fall, many of them, you know, become very beautifully colored. The variety of colors that you see in different trees is very pleasing to the eye. The maple-leaf is colored bright red, the oak a deep red, the walnut yellow, and other trees have their leaves variously colored.

Some trees change their leaves earlier than others, and some at first are only partly changed. So you see the green mingled beautifully with the bright red, yellow, and other colors. I have often admired a single tree standing by itself when it is partly changed. The maple is particularly beautiful. The top generally changes first. You often see the top bright red, and then the red is mixed with the green here and there in other parts of the tree. A little way off it looks as if the top were a cluster of red flowers. And the other parts of the tree look as if the flowers were coming out among the green leaves.

When the sun shines brightly all the different colors of the leaves make the woods look at a little distance as if they were all covered with blossoms. It is a very splendid sight that you see when you look off from a high hill over the woods on the hills and valleys. It looks as if monstrous bouquets of flowers had been stuck down thick together in the ground.

Such a sight is especially splendid when the sun is nearly down. Then the light and shade vary the scene. Here you see the top of a tall tree standing bright in the sun, while the other trees around are in the shade. There you see a whole cluster of tall trees lighted up on one side. Here is a shaded spot, and there, close by, is a very bright spot, the sun shining upon it through some break in a hill. The colors in the lighted spots look the brighter for the shaded spots near by.

So, too, it is very beautiful when, with the sun overhead, broken clouds are passing quickly in the sky. The swift shadows of the clouds give constant changes to the scene. One shadow seems to be chasing another over a bed of flowers.

When the leaves put on these bright colors it is the beginning of their death. They soon fall to the ground, and decay, and become a part of the earth. Some one has said that flowers are God's smiles. So we may say that God smiles upon us in the dying leaf, when he makes it so much like a flower.

How it is that all these different colors are made in the leaves in the autumn we know not. It is said that the frost makes them, but no one can tell how it does it. And, indeed, it is probably not the frost alone that thus paints the leaves, for the change sometimes begins before any frost is perceived. We do not understand how this effect is produced any better than we do how the various colors of the flowers are made.

It is singular that in England the leaves do not appear in these very bright colors in autumn, so that an Englishman is astonished at the beauty of our forests in that season of the year. Now why it is that the leaves are not affected there, in the same way that they are here, we do not know. It is supposed that it is because there is more dampness there than there is with us. Whatever may be the cause, it makes a great difference with the beauty of autumnal scenery. We should hardly be willing to exchange the brilliancy of an American October day for the dull colors presented by the forests in England.

Questions.—*Why* is autumn called the fall of the year? What are evergreens? What is told about quince-trees and currant-bushes? What is said of the colors of leaves just before they fall? Tell about the maple as its leaves are changing. How do the forests look in the bright sun when the leaves are changed? How do they look just before sundown? How when shadows of clouds are passing over them? What is said about God's making the dying leaves so much like flowers? Do we know how the colors are made in the leaves in autumn? What is said about the leaves in England?

CHAPTER XXII.

LEAF-BUDS.

L EAVES COME from buds just as flowers do. If you look at the buds in the spring on a tree you see that they are beginning to swell. They grow larger and larger, like the buds that turn into blossoms. After a while they unfold, and the green leaves are spread out.

How is it, you will want to know, that these leaves are made? They are very different from the leaves of the blossoms; but, like them, they are made out of the sap. The sap comes constantly to the leaf-bud, just as it does to the flower-bud, through the fine pipes in the stem. And so this sap is made into leaves.

There are, then, leaf-buds and flower-buds. You can tell them apart by their shapes. The flower-buds are round and short; the leaf-buds are long and pointed. You can see this difference very plainly on a peach-tree in the spring.

On some trees the flower-buds open before the leaf-buds. This is the case with some of the maples. The red color that makes them look so beautiful in the spring, before they have put out their leaves, is owing to the blossoms with which they are covered. These are quite small, and they are very rich, if you examine them with a microscope. The flower-buds of the peach-trees also open before the leaf-buds, and some of them are very splendid with their multitudes of pink blossoms.

There is sometimes another kind of buds. There are buds from which both leaves and flowers are formed. You see this in the lilac. The leaves first spread out from the bud, and then in the midst of the leaves comes out a cluster of flowers. When we see all these leaves and blossoms, and remember the bud, we wonder that so much can come out of so little a bud as this was.

This seems very wonderful when we see it in the horse-chestnut. I have often watched from day to day the buds of this tree as they were opening. You see at first a small bud covered with brown scales. It grows larger and larger day after day, and after a while appears as you see it here. Soon you see it open and the leaves push out. But they are all folded up. You see them unfold more and more every day. After a while there is a tall stalk with leaves having long stems. Then comes a large cluster of blossoms at the top of this stalk.

You can see the same thing in the grape-vine. The grape-stalk looks in winter as if it were a dead stick. It does not look as if any thing living could come out from it. But in the spring you see little buds starting out here and there. Watch one of these buds. You will see it swell, and after a while leaves will unfold from it. And you will see that what comes from the bud is not leaves alone. It is a branch with leaves on it. After a while clusters of blossoms appear among the leaves, filling the air with their fragrance. Then grapes form. The branch goes on to grow, and gets to be many feet long by the time the grapes are ripe. All this comes from the little bud, and is made out of the sap.

Now suppose you could see all this happen while you stand looking at the vine. Suppose you could see the bud swell, then the leaves push out, then the flowers form, then the grapes, and then see the whole grow while the grapes are growing and ripening. You would think this very wonderful. But it is just as wonderful to have all this done slowly. The great wonder is that it is done at all. No one but God could make all this come from a bud. And he

could do it in an hour as well as in several weeks if he thought it was best.

This unfolding of plants is very beautiful and interesting. I have often watched it in the rock-saxifrage, one of the wild flowers of spring. I have, for this purpose, taken it up with a little earth around it, when it was nothing but a small bud peeping up out of the ground, and have put it into a saucer. As I watched it from day to day the bud spread out into leaves. Then came up a little stalk out of the midst of the cluster of leaves, and on the end of the stalk appeared a great many little white flowers.

You see the same thing in the English cowslip, which is represented at the bottom of the opposite page. All this came from a little bud, just as it is with the rock-saxifrage. That curious but elegant plant, the crown-imperial, unfolds in a little different way. A stalk comes up in the midst of the leaves; but as it grows up leaves come out from the stalk. When it is fully grown, and in blossom, the whole plant presents a singular but splendid appearance. The long pointed leaves stand out around the tall, straight stalk for some way up. Then the stalk is naked for as much as the length of two fingers, and on the top is a crown of leaves and flowers, the flowers hanging down. It is very well named the crown-imperial.

But there are jewels in this crown that most people do not see. They are to be seen only by looking up into the flower. In each leaf of the flower where it joins on to the stem there is a beautiful little shallow cup which is very white. From this cup hangs a shining drop, like a tear. The whiteness of the cup gives the drop a rich pearly color. It seems, as you look up into the flower, as if there were six splendid pearls fastened there.

Each cup always has this drop hanging from it. If you put up something which will soak it up, there will soon be another one formed there. These drops are the honey of the flower.

Questions.—What do leaves come from? What are they made of? How can you tell the difference between flower-buds and leaf-buds? Mention some trees on which the flower-buds open before the leaf-buds. What is said about another kind of buds? Tell about the lilac—the horse-chestnut—the grape-vine. Would it be any more wonderful if the unfolding of the buds of the grape-vine were done in a shorter time? Tell about the rock-saxifrage—the English cowslip—the crown-imperial. What is very curious and beautiful in the crown-imperial?

CHAPTER XXIII.
THE COVERINGS OF THE BUDS.

YOU REMEMBER that I mentioned to you the brown scales on the buds of the horse-chestnut. I will tell you what these scales are for: they cover up the tender bud from the cold of winter and early spring. These scales are quite thick, as you can see. They are glued together, too, quite tightly by a sticky substance. They make in this way a close little case for the bud, to keep it snug from the cold air. When the weather gets warm enough the swelling bud pushes the scales apart. And when the leaves are out these scales drop off, because there is no more use for them.

In cold climates the buds are always protected in this way by a covering. The buds that you see in the spring do not begin in the spring. They are formed the year before, a little while before the leaves begin to fall. And as they form they loosen the leaves, and soon push them off.

Now in these little buds are locked up all the leaves and flowers that are to come out the next spring. The precious treasures of another year are in these buds. They must be kept safe, then, through the cold winter. And so they have tight coverings to guard them from the cold. They are all this time quite small, but they are ready to grow whenever the warm weather comes. If you should pick off the covering of one of these buds in the winter the cold air would freeze it, and it would die.

These coverings have been called by some one the "winter-cradles" of the buds. It is a very good name for them. The little buds in these cradles rock back and forth in the cold winds of winter, and are as secure from harm as the little baby in its cradle in its nice warm home, shut in from the wintry blasts.

And notice another thing. The inside of these cradles is lined with a soft down. This is the bud's little blanket to keep it warm in its cradle.

In warm climates the buds do not have these "winter-cradles," for there is no need of them. The buds of the orange-tree and lemon-tree have no coverings.

It is thus that God takes care of the tender bud. He always gives it a covering when it needs one to keep it from the cold. But in the sunny south he leaves the bud naked to the pleasant warm air. To put a thick covering over it there would do it harm. It would be like a man's putting on a heavy overcoat in mid-summer.

Questions.—*What* is said of the scales of the horse-chestnut bud? What is said of the buds in cold climates? Why is it very necessary to have the buds kept safe through the winter? What very good name has been given to the coverings of buds? How is it with the buds in warm climates? What is said of the care which God takes of buds?

CHAPTER XXIV.
WHAT ROOTS ARE FOR.

WHEN A seed sprouts, the root, I have told you, goes down into the ground, while the stalk goes upward into the air. The root goes down because the food of the plant is in the ground. It is the business of the root to suck up this food, so that the plant may be nourished and grow. The root is, then, a sort of stomach to the plant. If it had no root it would not grow, any more than you would if you had no stomach to put your food in.

The root has little mouths in its branches every where. It is by these that the food of the plant is sucked up. They are so small that you can not see them without a powerful microscope. They are in the fine parts or fibres of the root that you see hanging to the main branches of it when you take up a root. We are very careful not to break off these fibres when we take up a plant or tree to set it out again in another place; for the more of these little mouths there are, the more likely will it be to live. If all the fibres be broken off from the root the plant can not live, because there are no mouths to suck up the food. It will die just as you would if you should stop eating.

As there are little mouths all over the fibres of a root, there must be a multitude of them. You can not count them any more than you can count the sands on the seashore. These mouths drink up a fluid from the ground. This fluid is the sap that goes up in the stalk to nourish the plant. Every thing in the plant—the leaves, the flowers, the fruit—is made, as I have told you before, from the sap that the root sucks up.

These mouths do not suck up exactly the same thing in all roots. The sap of one plant differs somewhat from that of another plant. What the root of a pepper-plant sucks up is not the same that is sucked up by the root of a strawberry-plant. The root of the pepper-plant sucks up such sap that the biting peppers can be made out of it. And the root of the strawberry-plant sucks up sap that is fitted to make its pleasant fruit.

The pepper-plant and the strawberry-plant are so different from each other, that we should hardly suppose that they could grow out of the same earth side by side. But they can. How is this? Do the little mouths in the roots choose their food? They do. The strawberry mouths choose what will make strawberries, and the pepper mouths choose what will make peppers. But they do not choose in the same way that we choose. They do not think about it as we do. But they choose just as well as if they did think. Perhaps they choose better than we do. We sometimes make mistakes about our food. But they always choose just right. How this is we do not know. God has made them in such a way that they suck up the right kind of food from the earth. This is all that we know about it.

Very commonly different kinds of plants will grow in the same kind of earth. What a variety of plants and trees you often see in the same garden! But sometimes one plant requires a different soil from other plants. You see this in the asparagus. This vegetable does best in a soil that has considerable salt in it; that is, it thrives on salt food, as we may say. For this reason we sprinkle salt over an asparagus-bed in the spring.

But while salt makes the asparagus grow so well, it will kill other plants. It will kill all the weeds and grass that happen to be in the asparagus-bed. If you put on a good deal of salt no weeds will come up till after all the salt is sucked up by the asparagus. I had a chance last spring to see how bad salt is for grass. The man who put the salt on my asparagus-bed spilled some of it on a grassplot close by. In every spot where it fell it killed the grass. So you see that what is poison to grass is food to asparagus.

We find some kinds of flowers only in swamps. These will not grow well in the high grounds where the soil is different. The reason is, that the little mouths in the roots do not find the right kind of food there.

Questions.—*How* is the root a sort of stomach to a plant? Where are the little mouths of the root? What is said about care in moving plants or trees? What is said of the number of mouths in a root, and of their size? Do the roots of the pepper-plant and the strawberry-plant suck up the same kind of food? What is said of the mouths of roots choosing their food from the ground? Tell about the asparagus. What is said of plants growing in swamps?

CHAPTER XXV.

MORE ABOUT ROOTS.

THE ROOT, BESIDES being a sort of stomach to the plant, is its support. The plant is fastened by it firmly in the ground. For this reason a large tree has a large and deep root. Its root branches out very much as the tree does above. It is shaped as you see here. But when the plant is quite small, and there is not much to be supported, the root is different. It is perhaps made up of fibres as seen in this figure. This is the case with the roots of grass, as you can see by pulling up some of it. In a piece of turf there are a great many spears of grass, and so it is full of these fibrous roots mingled together.

Some roots are made for still another purpose. Besides nourishing the plant and supporting it, the root sometimes answers for food. When a root is intended for this use it is large. Look at the root of the beet. Here is a

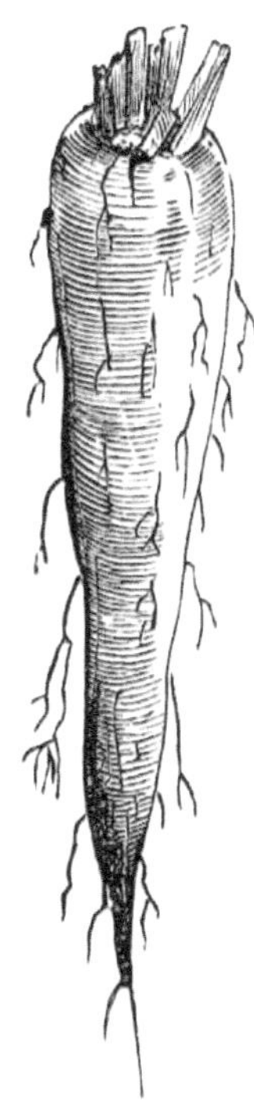

figure of it. The plant does not need so large a root as this to nourish and support it. The plant is nothing but a bunch of leaves, and with a very small root it would stand up in the ground. A small root, too, would answer to suck up all the sap that it needs. So small a plant could get along with a very small stomach.

You remember that in the chapter on seeds I told you that the seed-holder is sometimes larger than it need be to hold the seeds. The pear is a seed-holder, but it is larger than it need be if it were meant to be only a seed-holder. It is meant to be something else. It is fruit to be eaten as well as a seed-holder. It answers two purposes. So, too, when a root is larger than it need be to nourish the plant, it answers two purposes. Besides sucking up food for the plant, it answers as food for animals.

In these large roots the mouths that suck up the sap are not in the body of the root. They are in the little fibres that are joined on to the main root, as you see in the beet. In the root of the turnip, as seen in this figure, there is a sort of tail going down into the ground from the bottom of it. The fibres, where the mouths are, make a part of this tail.

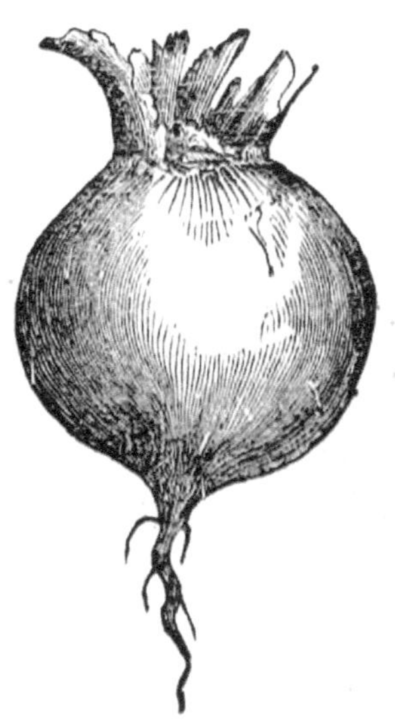

In some plants roots are formed very curiously. Shoots start out and run along on the ground. After a little while these runners, as they are called, send down roots into the ground, as is here represented. The strawberry, you know, spreads in this way. So do the verbenas. When a runner gets fairly rooted it can live by itself, for it has a root, that is, a stomach of its own. You can separate it now from the main plant if you choose, and set it out somewhere else. This is done whenever we plant a new strawberry-bed.

This is a singular kind of root. It is spread out like a hand. Each of these fingers can be separated from the rest, and will grow by itself. The roots of the dahlias are of this kind.

Some roots are bulbs, as they are called. The onion is a bulbous root. Below is one cut open. You see that it is all made up of coats, one inside of another, which you can peel off. The roots of hyacinths, lilies, blue-

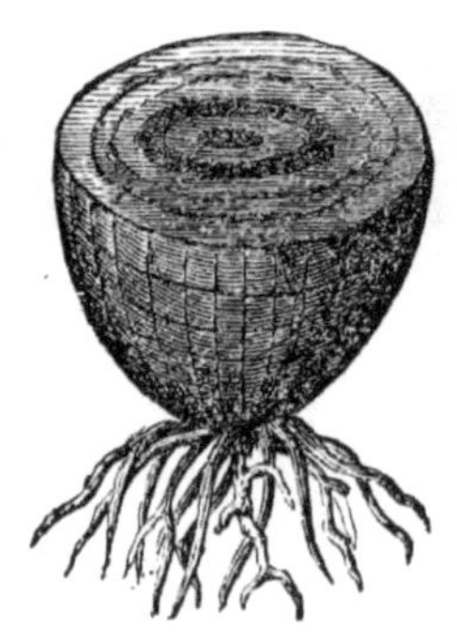

bells, and crocuses, are bulbs. These lie in the earth very still through all the winter. The life in them is asleep, just as it is in the buds. But it wakes up in the spring, and down go the roots from the bottom of the bulbs, and up come the plants from their tops. It is sometimes said that a bulb is really a bud, only it is in the ground, instead of being in the air as most buds are. Thus the onion is a bud, and the real roots of the plant are what you see branching down from the bottom of the bulb.

You have heard people talk about setting out slips. A slip is a branch of a plant. Some plants will grow from slips. Geraniums will. If you put a slip of geranium into the ground and keep it well watered, a root will shoot down into the earth from the end of the stem. And so the branch cut off becomes a growing plant. Before it was cut off it got its food with the other branches from the root of the plant to which it belonged. After it was cut off it could not live unless it could get a root of its own to suck up its food from the ground.

Most plants get their food from the ground. But some do not. Some get their food from water. This is the case with a plant called duck-meat, that is found in ponds and ditches where the water is still. You see little leaves on the surface of the water, and the roots hang like threads from the leaves. This is represented in this figure. Now there is something in the water in these places which is sucked up by these roots and makes the leaves grow. Sea-weed has no roots extending down into the ground, but it gets its nourishment from the water.

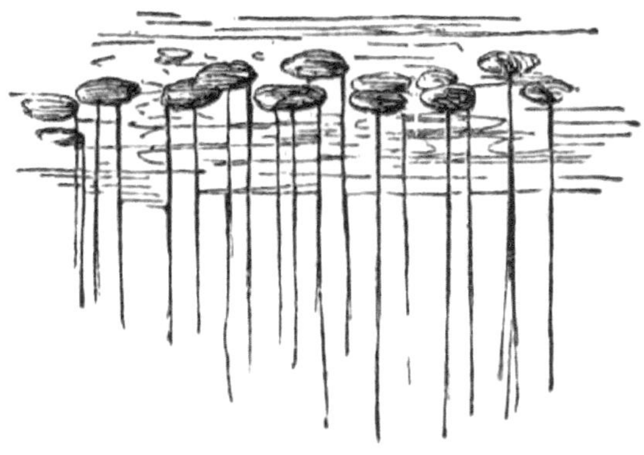

There are some plants that live on other plants. The mosses that you see on trees are plants of this kind. At the South there is a kind of gray moss that hangs down from the branches of trees, sometimes to a great length. It makes the land look as if it were hung in mourning. The sap that nourishes this plant it gets from the bark of the trees. There are mouths in the moss where it hangs from the tree that suck in the sap which they find there.

The dodder, or love-vine, is a curious plant. It lives on other plants. It comes up out of the ground and clings to any plant that happens to be near it. After it is well fastened, and has grown considerably, its root in the ground dies. The little vine does not need it any longer, for it clings by real roots to the plant up which it runs. This is the reason that it is called love-vine; for, like love, it lives on that to which it clings. This vine has no leaves, and it is of a bright-yellow color. So it is sometimes called gold-thread vine.

Questions.—*What* is said about the root as a support for a tree? How is it with the roots of grass? What is said about roots that are for food? Tell about the root of the beet. Give the comparison made between roots and seed-holders. What is said of the root of the turnip? What of the roots of strawberries and verbenas? What of the roots of dahlias? What is said of bulbs? How do plants grow from slips? What is said about the duck-meat? What is said of mosses? Tell about the dodder.

CHAPTER XXVI.
STALKS AND TRUNKS.

WE SPEAK of plants as having stalks, and of trees as having trunks. A tree has a stout firm trunk, because its top is so large and heavy. Its branches spread out so much, that the tree would be broken down by the wind if it did not have a strong trunk.

It is the woody part of the trunk that is so strong. The stalks of plants have no wood in them, because they do not need it. They are strong enough to support the branches without having any wood in them.

Some plants have their stalks made strong in a singular way. There is a flinty earth in them. This is the case with wheat, and rye, and most kinds of grass. See how tall the stalk of rye or wheat is. And it is very slender. But as the wind bends it over it does not break, because the flint in it makes it so strong.

It is this flint in different kinds of straws that fits them to be used in making hats and bonnets. They would not be firm enough for this use if there was no flint in them.

You can not see or feel the flint in the straw. The reason is, that the particles of the flint are so fine, and are so well mixed up with the fibres or threads of the straw. It is this fine flint in straw that makes its ashes so useful in polishing marble. In some plants you can feel the roughness that is made by the flint. You can feel it in the scouring-rush, which is sometimes used by house-keepers in scouring. In this there is more of the stony substance than there is in the straw of your hat, and it is not as fine.

But you will ask how stone or flint gets into these plants. It is sucked up from the ground by the mouths in the roots, and it goes up in the sap to where it is wanted. It is wanted in the stalk of the grain, and so it stops there. It never makes a mistake by going into the kernels of the grain. If it did, the flour that is made from them would be gritty, as we should find out when we came to eat the bread.

All plants that have no wood in their stalks die down to the ground in the autumn, though the roots of some of them live through the winter. But trees, you know, remain from year to year. So do shrubs and bushes. These may be considered as little trees. Some shrubs are so small that they do not need to have their stalks woody merely to support the branches. Thus the currant-bush could have its branches well supported if the stalks were not woody. In such cases the stalks are made woody so that they may last over the winter.

Stalks and trunks commonly stand up of themselves. But there are some that can not. When this is so we call the plant a vine. Vines are supported in various ways. Some are held up by merely winding around something. This is true of the bean-vine. It winds itself, as it grows, around the pole that is put up for it. The hop-vine is supported in the same way. It is, you know, quite rough, and so it can cling firmly even to quite a smooth pole.

Pea-vines are held up in a different way. Little tendrils are put forth which wind around the branches of the bushes that are set for the vines to run up on. These tendrils clasp very tightly. You see them on many kinds of vines. You see them on grape-vines, and on the vine of the passion-flower. Sometimes the tendrils go out from the ends of the leaves. You see a leaf of this kind on page 68.

A vine called thunbergia is held up in a very queer manner. If a leaf happens to come near a twig or a string it twists its stem around it. So the stems of the leaves act as tendrils to support the vine.

The vine of the trumpet-creeper is supported in a singular way. Whenever it touches any thing there come out at the joints of the stalks some sprawling things like the feet of a spider. These feet fasten themselves very strongly to whatever the vine is running on. If it runs up the side of a board fence, these feet mix up their fibres very tightly with the fibres of the wood. It is curious to observe that where any part of the vine is not against any thing these feet do not appear. They are made only where they can be used. The plant acts just as if it knew where it could use them.

Questions.—What is the difference between stalks and trunks? Why does a tree need so strong a trunk? Why do the stalks of plants have no wood in them? What is said of the flinty earth that is in some of them? In what ways is the flint in straws of use? What is said of the scouring-rush? How does flint get into any plant? Why does it not go into the kernels of grain as well as into the stalks? What becomes of stalks that are not woody in the winter? What is said of the woody stalks of shrubs? What are vines? How is the bean-vine supported? Tell about tendrils. What is said of the thunbergia? Describe the way in which the trumpet-creeper is supported.

CHAPTER XXVII.

THE BARK OF TREES AND SHRUBS.

IN THE trunk of a tree or the stalk of a shrub there are three parts. They are the bark, the wood, and the pith.

The bark is not all one thing. It is made up of two parts; or rather, we should say, there are two barks. There is an outer bark and an inner one. The outer bark has no life in it. It is this outer bark that gives such a roughness to the trunks of some trees, as the elm and the oak. In the birch, you can peel off this bark in strips right around the trunk of the tree. Indians make very pretty boxes of these strips of birch-bark.

The outer bark is a *coat* for the tree. It covers up the living parts so that they shall not be injured. It does for the tree what our clothes do for our bodies. It is not a perfectly tight coat. It has little openings every where in it. It would be bad for the tree to have this coat on it tight, just as it would be bad for our bodies to have an India-rubber covering close to the skin.

This outer bark is a great protection to the tree through the cold winter. It keeps the cold from killing the trunk and the branches. This coat of the tree covers it all, even out to the end of the smallest twig. The tree looks as if it was dead in winter without its green leaves. But there is life locked up there, just as I told you there is in the seed that is kept through the winter. The life in the tree is asleep as it is in the seed. It is ready to be waked up when the warm weather of the spring shall come. During this winter's sleep of the tree, the living inner bark and wood are safe, covered up by the tree's rough coat.

If you peel off the outer bark, as you can very easily in the birch, you come to the fresh and juicy inner bark. This I have told you is alive. It is full of sap. It has a great deal to do with the growth of the tree. It is by this bark that the wood inside of it is made.

You have sometimes seen small trees covered in the winter with straw tied nicely all around them. This is because they are tender trees that are not used to our cold weather. They belong to a warmer climate, and God gave them just such a coat as they needed there. And when we undertake to have such trees here at the north, the coat that God has given them is not enough to keep them from freezing in our long, cold winters. So we have to put another coat over it.

Questions.—What are the parts of the trunk of a tree? Tell about the bark. What is the outside bark for? How much of the tree does it cover and protect? What is said of the life asleep in the trees in the winter? What is said of the inner bark? Why is straw tied around some trees in winter?

CHAPTER XXVIII.

THE WOOD IN TREES AND SHRUBS.

PERHAPS IT seemed strange to you when I said in the last chapter that bark makes wood. But so it is. Every year the living inner bark goes to work and makes a layer of wood out of the sap that is in it. This work is done in the warm weather. In the winter there is no wood made. The tree is asleep then.

It is what the bark does that makes the tree larger every year. A new layer of wood is formed by it all up the trunk, and along out to the end of all the branches.

The different layers of wood made in the different years are often very distinct from each other. You can see 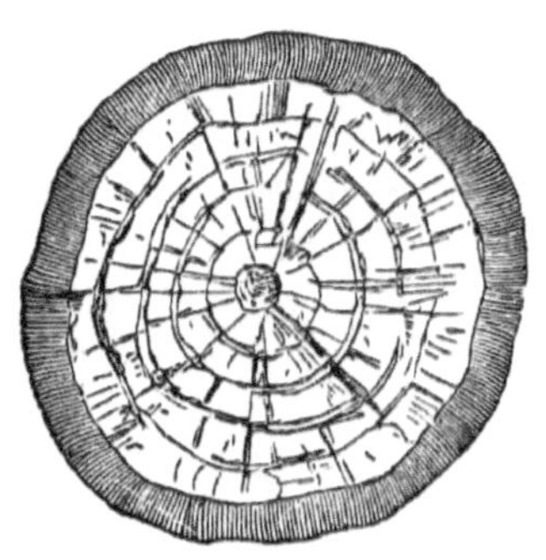 them in a log that has been cut or sawn across. Sometimes they are so distinct that you can count them, and so tell just how many years old the tree is. Here is a representation of the sawn end of the trunk of a tree. You see that the rings of the wood are very plain.

The wood part of the trunk and branches is full of small pipes. It is through these pipes that the sap goes up from the roots and gets to the leaves. It is in this way that it goes to the very ends of the topmost boughs of the tallest trees. This is very wonderful. How the sap is made to go up such a great distance through these pipes in the wood we do not know. There is only one way that man can make water go so high through pipes.

He can do it by a forcing-pump. But we can see nothing like forcing-pumps in the trees. We find nothing but these pipes going from the roots up to the leaves. And the sap is flowing up through them very quietly all the time.

In a large tree there is a multitude of these pipes in the wood. And when you look at the huge trunk, think what a quantity of sap there is going up through it all the time to keep all those leaves fresh and green. If you could see it all in one pipe it would be quite a stream.

If you look at the end of a log you will see that there are two kinds of wood. The wood in the centre is different from that which is around it. It is called the heart-wood. The pipes in it are stopped up, and no sap can go up through it. The pipes for the sap are clear only in the newest part of the wood.

The use of the pith of trees and plants we do not understand. The pith is very small in trees, but it is quite large in some plants and shrubs. All boys know that it is very large in the elder. It is also large in the stalks of corn, and of the sugar-cane.

Questions.—*How* is the wood in a tree made? What is said of the different layers of wood? What is said of the small pipes in the wood? Do we know how the sap is made to go up in them? What is said of the quantity of sap that goes up in the trunk of a large tree? What is said of the two kinds of wood that you see in looking at the end of a log? What do we know about the pith of trees and plants?

CHAPTER XXIX.

WHAT IS MADE FROM SAP.

EVERY THING that you see in a tree or a plant is made from the sap. The bark, the wood, the leaves, the flowers, the fruit, are all made from it. Even the root that sucks up the sap from the ground is made from the sap itself.

It is strange that so many different things can be made out of the same thing. It is strange that a rough bark and hard wood can be made from the same thing as the beautiful flower and the delicious fruit. Look at an apple-blossom, and then look at the bark of the tree, and think of them as being made from the same sap. You can hardly believe that it is so. How strange it is to think of the sharp thorns on a rose-bush as being made from the same sap that makes the soft, and smooth, and beautiful leaves of the roses!

If any man should tell you that he could make a brick and a piece of cloth, with beautifully colored figures on it, from the same thing, you would say he was crazy. But there is not as much difference between the brick and the cloth as there is between rude bark and a flower made from the same sap. The Creator does, in the most common plants and trees, what man can not equal in any way.

There are some things made from sap that I have said nothing about as yet. There are many bitter, and sweet, and sour things made from sap. Sometimes sweet and bitter things are made at the same time from the same sap. You see this in the orange. From the same sap that comes to the orange through the stem are made the sweet juice and the sharp and bitter peel.

Almost all our sugar comes from the sugar-cane. This is shaped like the stalks of corn. The sugar is made from the sap that comes up in the pipes of the cane from the ground. The cane, then, is really a sugar-factory. Man does not make the sugar, but it is made for him in the cane. It is in the juice of the cane. This juice is mostly sugar and water. In making sugar, as it is called, the sugar is not made. It is only separated from the water and other things with which it is mixed in the cane.

The sugar is made from the cane in this way. The cane is cut into pieces, and these are put into a mill where they are pressed between iron rollers. The juice squeezed out in the mill runs off into a large reservoir or tub in the boiling-house. It is now put into boilers and boiled down. In this boiling the water goes off in steam, but the sugar remains. When it is boiled down to a sirup it is put into very large wooden trays called coolers. Here the sirup becomes sugar, because the rest of the water goes off in the air.

The way in which sugar is made perfectly white, it is said, was discovered in a curious way. A hen that had gone through a clay mud-puddle went with her muddy feet into a sugar-house. She left her tracks on a pile of sugar. It was observed by some one that wherever her tracks were the sugar was whitened. This led to some experiments. The result was, that wet clay came to be used in refining sugar. It is used in this way. The sugar is put into earthen jars shaped as you see the sugar-loaves are. The large ends are upward. The small ends have a hole in them. Here is a picture of one of these jars. The clay is put on the top of the sugar in the large end of the jar, and it is kept wet. The moisture goes down through the sugar, and drops from the

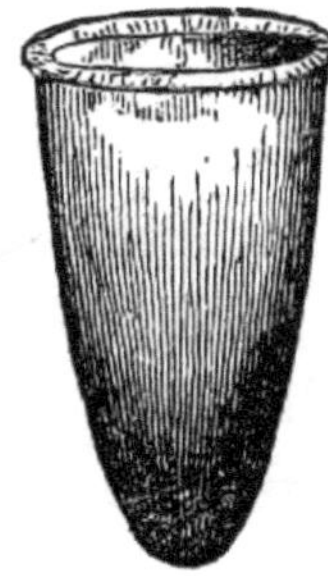

hole in the small end of the jar. This makes the sugar perfectly white.

This discovery shows how much a little looking and thinking will together do. What the hen did was a small thing. One would hardly suppose that any thing could be learned from a hen's tracks. Most people would have scraped off the mud from the pile of sugar, and thought nothing more of it. But the man who saw the tracks was in the habit of thinking about what he saw. And so he discovered in that hen's tracks a very useful fact. If you always think about what you see you may some time be a discoverer too. At any rate, that is the way to learn. And it is to help you in learning to think about what you see that I have written this book.

Questions.—*What* things are made from sap? Mention some things very different from each other that are made from the same sap. Give the comparison about brick and cloth. What is said about the orange? What about the sugar-cane? How is sugar made from the sugar-cane? Of what use is the boiling? Tell how one way of purifying sugar was discovered. What does this discovery show?

CHAPTER XXX.

MORE ABOUT WHAT IS MADE FROM SAP.

YOU HAVE eaten maple-sugar. This comes from a tree called the sugar-maple. The sugar is in the sap, just as it is in the case of the sugar-cane. The sap is obtained early in the spring by tapping the trees, and then it is boiled down, as it is called. In this boiling the water goes off in steam and the sugar remains. The sugar-maple, then, is a sugar-factory as well as the sugar-cane.

There are many roots in which there is sugar. Sugar has often been obtained from a kind of beet called the sugar-beet. There is sugar in many fruits, making them sweet to the taste.

Now where does the sugar in the sugar-cane, the maple, the beet, etc., come from? The sap in which the sugar is comes up from the roots. You will say, then, that the little mouths in the roots suck up sugar from the ground. But there is no sugar in the ground. No one ever found any there. Take up a handful of earth, smell of it, and taste of it. There is no sweetness in it.

Though there is no sugar in the ground, what the sugar is made from is there. This the little mouths in the root drink up, and it is made into sugar in the plant. You see, then, how true it is that the plant is a sugar-factory.

Now do you think that any man could in any way make sugar from the earth under his feet? He can no more do it than he can make a flower or a leaf.

There are a great many other things made by plants

from what they suck up from the earth. I will mention some of them.

Some plants are starch-factories. They make the starch from the sap that comes up from the root, just as the sugar is made. There is starch in every kind of grain, in potatoes, and in many other roots.

Some plants are medicine-factories. Camphor is obtained from the bark and wood of a tree. Opium is found in the different kinds of poppies. There are various bitter medicines that are found in different plants. Castor-oil is obtained from the seeds of a large plant. These, and various other medicines, are made from sap.

Some plants are gum-factories. You have sometimes seen gum on the bark of peach-trees and cherry-trees, when the bark has been wounded in some way. Now there are some kinds of trees in which there is a great deal of gum. The India rubber is a gum that is obtained from some kinds of trees in warm climates. When the bark of these trees is wounded this gum oozes out. It is collected as it flows. It is dried in smoke, and this gives it its dark appearance.

Many plants are perfume-factories, as I told you in Chapter V. The perfumes are made most often in the flowers, but they are sometimes made in the leaves and other parts. You know how fragrant the leaves of the geranium are. Even wood is sometimes fragrant. The sandal-wood is very much so.

Some plants are color-makers. They not only make colors for their own use—that is, to color their flowers—but they make them for us to use. Many of our dyes with which we color cloths come from plants. They are made in the plants from the sap that comes up from the ground. It seems strange that the blue indigo should be made out of what a plant drinks up from the brown, dull earth. But so it is.

Now just think over the various things that are made from the sap in plants. There are wood, bark, leaves, flowers, fruits, thorns, perfumes, colorings, sugar, starch, gum, various medicines, etc. And then there are many other things that I have not mentioned. How strange it is that so many and such different things can be made from what the plants suck up out of the earth! As you look at the ground under your feet, you can hardly believe that so much can be got out of it. It is the busy little mouths in the roots that get from it what is needed to make all these different things.

Questions.—*What* is said of the sugar-maple? What is said of sugar in some roots and fruits? As there is no sugar in the ground, how does it get into plants? Can any body make sugar from earth? What plants are starch-factories? Mention some medicines made in plants. What is said about plants that are gum-makers? What is said about perfumes being made in plants? What about colors? What is said about indigo? Mention now all the things that you can think of that are made from the sap in plants.

CHAPTER XXXI.
CIRCULATION OF THE SAP.

I HAVE told you that the sap goes up in a plant or a tree in certain pipes. Now when it gets to the leaves it turns about and goes back again down toward the ground by some other pipes.

So there is a set of pipes for the sap to go up, and a set of pipes for it to go down. In a tree, the pipes for it to go up are in the wood. Now where do you think the pipes are for it to go down? They are in the live part of the bark. The sap is all the time going up to the leaves in the one set of pipes, and coming down in the other set. And this is what we call the circulation of the sap.

The sap that goes up has a great deal of water in it. Much of this water is got rid of when the sap comes to the leaves. You remember that I told you, in the chapter on leaves, that water is let off into the air from their pores. For this reason the sap that comes down from the leaves has much less water in it than the sap that goes up.

The sap that goes up is not perfect sap. It has to make a visit to the leaves and get an airing there before it can be of much use. After it is aired it goes to all parts of the plant, down to the very roots.

It is this aired sap from which generally every part of the plant grows, or is made. You remember that I told you in the last chapter that in trees the inner bark makes a new layer of wood every year. Now the bark makes the wood from some of this aired sap as it goes down in the pipes of the bark.

You remember that I told you in the chapter on leaves, that they have much to do with the growth of a plant. You can now see why this is so. The sap has to go up to the leaves to be made good sap. Just what the air does to it there you are not yet old enough to understand. But after a little time you will be able to understand this, and then you will see that leaves are very properly called the lungs of plants, and that they breathe with them as we do with our lungs, though in a different manner.

I have said that the sap that goes up is not of much use, and that every thing in the plant is made from the sap that goes down. This is not always so. In the sugar-maple it is the sap that goes up in the early spring that has the sugar in it. The sugar-gatherers tap the trees before the leaves are put forth. The leaves, then, have nothing to do with making the sugar. How it is made we can not understand. We suppose that it is done in the root, where the mouths are that drink up the sap from the earth. But though we do not know how it is, in some way every sugar-maple as soon as it begins to be warmed by the air of spring becomes at once a sugar-factory.

Though most of our sugar comes from the sugar-cane of southern climates, a great deal is made from the sap of the sugar-maple in some parts of the northern and western states in this country. A very busy time they have in some places in the early spring in collecting the sap and in boiling it down. The sirup is often sold as maple-sugar molasses. But more often it is made into sugar; and great quantities of it are sold every year. In some places where it is made many of the people use no other sugar.

The sap is all the time in motion in the trees and plants in all the warmer months of the year. It is always going up and coming down. It does so till the leaves fall and the cold of winter comes. Then all this motion stops. And through the winter the sap is almost as still as if the trees and shrubs were dead. Then when the spring comes, the mouths in the roots begin again to suck up sap from the ground, and it runs up and down in the little pipes as it did the year before.

As you look at all the trees and plants about you, think how much sap there is running up and down in their pipes. Look at a very large tree, and think of this. In multitudes of pipes in that huge trunk the sap goes up to the very end of all the branches to the leaves, and then it comes down in other pipes. How wonderful this is, and yet how few there are that ever think about it!

Questions.—*Where* are the pipes in which the sap goes up in a tree? Where are the pipes in which it comes down? What is said about the water in the sap? What becomes of a part of this water? Why is it necessary for the sap to go up to the leaves? Are things made from the sap that goes up, or that which comes down? How is it with the sugar in the maple? Where is its sugar made? Is the sap always in motion?

CHAPTER XXXII.

THE SLEEP AND THE DEATH OF PLANTS.

WHEN THE cold weather comes some plants die, and some go to sleep for the winter.

Some plants always die in the fall. Corn dies; so does the bean-vine. And so do many other plants. In order to have such plants another year, we keep some of their seeds to put into the ground in the spring.

But some plants sleep in the winter. Look at a tree. Its branches are all bare. It seems as if it had no life in it. But there is life there, and it will show itself next spring. Its life is asleep, just as I told you it is in the seed before it is put into the ground. Its sap is all quiet in the pipes. The mouths in the roots have stopped their busy work. The buds all over the tree are asleep in their "winter-cradles." The wind rocks them back and forth, but never wakes them up.

How much life there is asleep in that tree! The buds are all there which are to make all that you will see on it the next summer. They are covered up snugly from the cold in their winter coats. The little things are very still, but they are alive. They only want a warm sun to make them show it. As soon in the spring as they feel the warmth through their coats, they begin to swell, as I have told you in another chapter, and soon open their coats and go to work to make leaves, and flowers, and fruits. A great work they do after their long winter sleep. Look up into a tree in summer and see how these leaf-buds have filled every branch with leaves. You can hardly believe that it is the same tree that you saw so bare in the winter.

Some plants die down to the ground, and their roots live through the winter. You know that this is the way with tulips and daffodils. They come up in the spring from the roots that have been in the ground all the winter. So, too, do the beautiful crocuses, that peep up so early in spring that they often get covered with snow. The roots of grass, too, live in the earth through the winter.

The life in these roots is asleep through the winter, just as it is in the trees and bushes. Their little mouths do not drink up any sap. How much life there is asleep in the winter covered up in the earth!

What do you think becomes of all the leaves that fall, and of all the plants that die in the autumn? They are not lost. They decay and become a part of the earth. A great deal of the ground under your feet was once in the shape of stalks, and leaves, and flowers. And now the roots suck up from it sap to be made into the same shapes again. So you see that the dead plants and leaves of one year are used in making the plants and leaves of the years that come after.

Questions.—*What* is said of plants that die in the fall? Tell how it is with a tree in the winter. What does the warm weather do to its buds in the spring? Mention some plants that die down to the ground in the fall, but whose roots live through the winter. What is said of the life in these roots? What effect does the spring have on them? What becomes of all the leaves and plants that die in the fall?